# So Wrong It
# Must Be Right

**Also by Nicole Helm**

*Mile High Romances:*

*Need You Now*

*Mess With Me*

*Want You More*

*Gallagher & Ivy Romances:*

*So Wrong It Must Be Right*

*So Bad It Must Be Good*

# So Wrong It Must Be Right

## Nicole Helm

LYRICAL PRESS
Kensington Publishing Corp.
www.kensingtonbooks.com

LYRICAL PRESS BOOKS are published by

Kensington Publishing Corp.
119 West 40th Street
New York, NY 10018

All Kensington titles, imprints, and distributed lines are available at special quantity discounts for bulk purchases for sales promotion, premiums, fund-raising, educational, or institutional use.

Special book excerpts or customized printings can also be created to fit specific needs. For details, write or phone the office of the Kensington Sales Manager: Kensington Publishing Corp., 119 West 40th Street, New York, NY 10018. Attn. Sales Department. Phone: 1-800-221-2647.

Lyrical Press and Lyrical Press logo Reg. U.S. Pat. & TM Off.

First Electronic Edition: March 2017
eISBN-13: 978-1-60183-962-6
eISBN-10: 1-60183-962-6

First Print Edition: March 2017
ISBN-13: 978-1-60183-963-3
ISBN-10: 1-60183-963-4

Printed in the United States of America

*To all the places I've lost, and all I've gained because of it.*

# Chapter 1

"You're not still emailing with that guy!"

Dinah looked up from her phone and blinked at her cousin. It took a minute to get her bearings and remember that Kayla was waiting on her to get started.

"Actually I was reading up on Trask. I found an article that might explain his reluctance to sell."

Kayla snatched Dinah's phone away, then frowned at the screen. "It is sick that you get the same look on your face reading those pervy emails as you do reading stuff for work."

"I don't know what you're talking about," Dinah replied primly. Okay, maybe she did know what Kayla meant, and maybe it was a little sick, but Gallagher's Tap Room was Dinah's blood. The Gallagher family had moved to St. Louis over a century ago, and built a little pub on the very land beneath the concrete floor under her feet. It was everything to her, and yeah, she got a little excited about that.

Kayla gestured toward the back door and Dinah stood to follow. Meeting with Trask was going to be the moment she finally proved to Uncle Craig and the board she was ready to take over as director of operations.

Being Uncle Craig's "special assistant" had turned out to mean little more than being his bitch, and while she'd worked to be the best damn bitch she could be, she was ready for tradition to take over. From the very beginning, the eldest Gallagher in every generation took over. These days, the title was director of operations, but it was all the same. And she was the eldest Gallagher of the eldest Gallagher. She'd been told her whole life Gallagher's would be hers when her father retired, or, as it turned out to be with Dad, abandoned everyone and everything in the pursuit of his midlife crisis.

It was time. Dinah was ready, and getting some crazy urban farmer to sell his land next to Gallagher's for the expansion was going to be the final point in her favor. No one would be able to deny she was ready.

Director of operations was everything she'd been dreaming about since she was old enough to understand what the job required. Long after she'd understood what Gallagher's meant to her family, and to her.

"So, you finally stopped emailing creepy Internet dude?"

Dinah walked with Kayla down the hallway to the back exit. "He's not creepy." The guy she'd randomly started emailing with, after she'd tipsily commented on his Tumblr page one night, wasn't creepy. He was kind of amazing.

"Dinah."

"I'm sorry. No way I'm giving that guy up. It's some of the hottest sex I've ever had."

Dinah thought wistfully about how he'd ended his last email. *And when you're at the point you don't think you can come again, I'll make sure that you do.* It might be only through a computer, but it was far superior to anything any other guy had ever said to her.

"It's fictional."

"So?"

"He's probably like a sixty-year-old perv. Or a woman, if he's really as good as you say he is."

"As you pointed out, it's fictional. Who cares?"

They stepped out into the lingering warmth of late September. The urban landscape around Gallagher's was a mix of old and new, crumbling and modern. Soon, Gallagher's was going to make sure the entire block was a testament to a city that could reinvent itself.

"What does he do, send you pictures of models? Oh, baby, check out my six-pack. Then suddenly he's claiming to be David Gandy."

"We don't trade pictures of each other or any personal information that might identify us. I mean, he knows I have freckles. I know he has a birthmark on his inner thigh, but that's about it. It is pure, harmless, sexy sexy words."

"Geez." Kayla waved her phone in front of Dinah's face, the screen displaying a myriad of apps. "Not even Snapchat?"

"Nope. It's all very old-fashioned. Like Jane Austen. Or *You've Got Mail.* Only with sex stuff."

"Go have some real sex, Dinah."

"I do that too!" Although admittedly less and less. Maybe not for six months or so. Trying to prove herself to Uncle Craig was eating her life away, and the nice thing about a sexy email was she could read it whenever she wanted and didn't have to remember its birthday or cook it dinner. It was perfect really, except the whole do-it-yourself aspect.

But do-it-yourself had been instilled in her from a young age, no matter how false the message rang in her adulthood.

The tract of land behind Gallagher's that Uncle Craig wanted to buy was a strange sight in downtown St. Louis. Between one empty lot Uncle Craig had already bought, and an aging home with a scraggly yard that Craig was also after, a land of green emerged.

Not even green grass, but huge plants, archways covered in leaves, rows and rows of produce-bearing stems. So much green stuff the crumbling brick exterior of the old house behind it all was barely visible from where they stood in front of the chain-link fence that enclosed the property.

"It's cute," Kayla observed from their vantage point on the cracked sidewalk. "Kind of funny we're trying to get him to sell it so we can pave over it and then have a farmers' market."

Dinah had waged her own personal battle over the seemingly ironic— or at the very least incongruous—business plan her uncle had put forth, but being the black sheep of the family, thanks to her dad screwing up just about everything, meant Dinah didn't have a say. Even Kayla, as sustainability manager, adding her opinion had done nothing to sway her father.

So, Dinah would find a way to get Mr. Hippie Urban Farmer to sell his land, and with any luck, convince him she was doing *him* a favor and sign him up for a booth for next year's market, which Kayla would be in charge of. The Gallagher & Ivy Farmers' Market would be a success one way or another.

"From what I can find, Trask grew up on a real farm and his family left that one, then he worked on the farm of some other family member, who sold to a developer or something. This place was his grandmother's house, and over the course of the past four years he's turned it into this. So, that may explain his refusing your father's initial offer," Dinah said.

"What makes you think we can get through to him if my dad couldn't?"

"His family has a history of selling land. He should be well versed in the benefits. Surely a guy like him wants a bigger space, and the money we're offering will allow him that. Besides, we have a soul and decency on our side."

Kayla snorted. "No offense, but I'm a little glad your dad went off the deep end and I'm not the only one with a soulless Gallagher as a father."

"Gee, thanks," Dinah muttered, trying to ignore the little stab of pain. She couldn't be offended at the attack on her dad. It was warranted. They'd spent plenty of their childhood complaining about Kayla's dad being a douche. But, still, it hurt. It wasn't supposed to be this way.

Oh well, what could she do? She and Kayla stepped under the archway of green tendrils and the sign that read *Front Yard Farm*. The place *was* cute. Weird, no doubt, but cute.

Before they could make it past the first hurdle of beanstalks or whatever, the door to the brick house creaked open and a man stepped onto the porch. Dinah stopped midstep, barely registering that Kayla did too.

He was tall and lanky and wore loose-fitting khaki-colored pants covered in dirt, and a flannel shirt with sleeves rolled to the elbows over a faded T-shirt. It was the face though that really caught her attention. Sharp and angular. Fierce. Only softened by the slight curl to his dark hair, his beard obscuring his jawline. Something about the way he moved was pure grace, and everything about his looks made Dinah's attraction hum to attention.

"He's like every hipster fantasy I've ever had, come to life," Dinah whispered, clutching Kayla's arm briefly.

"Lord, yes."

The man on the stoop, with the hoe, and the flannel, and the beard— sweet Lord—stared at them suspiciously. "Can I help you two?"

Dinah exchanged a glance with her cousin, who was valiantly trying to pretend they hadn't been drooling.

"Mr. Trask?"

"Yeah."

"Hi, I'm Dinah Gallagher and this is Kayla Gallagher. We're from Gallagher's Ta—"

"Nope."

The door slammed so emphatically, Dinah jerked back. She'd

barely registered the guy moving inside before he disappeared behind that slammed door.

"Well."

"What were you saying about human decency and souls making a difference?"

Dinah started picking her way across the narrow and uneven brick path to the door. "He hasn't had a chance to see it yet. Maybe the meeting with your dad ended poorly. We'll have to mend a few fences."

"Before we buy them all," Kayla muttered. "Remember when we were kids and thought we'd be calling the shots?"

"We still will be. Just need another decade." Or two. That's how family business worked. She wasn't going to abandon her destiny just because it was harder than she'd expected or taking longer than she'd anticipated. No, she was going to fight.

And should Kayla, her cousin and best friend, ever get married, Dinah would not follow in her father's footsteps and sleep with Kayla's spouse.

Dinah reached the door and knocked. She didn't entertain thoughts of failing because it simply wasn't an option. Failing Gallagher's was never going to be an option.

The door remained closed. Dinah pursed her lips. This was *not* going the way she'd planned.

"Okay. Well. I won't be deterred."

"Come on, Dinah. Let's go." Kayla stood in the yard, hands shoved into the pockets of her dress. "Call him. Write him an email. I don't want him calling the cops on us. Oh, maybe you can accidentally write him one of your sex emails. That'll get his attention." She sighed, loud enough to be heard across the yard. "I would so not mind getting that guy's attention."

"I'm going to pick something." Dinah surveyed the plants surrounding her. She didn't know a lot about farmers or farming, but if he was so dead set on not selling, he obviously cared deeply about this yard of produce. So, she'd lure him out that way.

"Don't! He'll call the cops."

Dinah waved her off. "I'll pick something ripe and give it back to him. I'm doing him a favor, really."

Kayla muttered a disagreement, but Dinah ignored her. She surveyed the arches of green and splashes of color—squash maybe.

The yard looked very familiar. Like she'd seen it . . . somewhere. Somewhere. Well, she didn't have time to dwell on that. She had to find a ripe vegetable to pick.

And since she had to no idea what she was doing, that was going to be a challenge.

Carter was not falling for this dirty trick. He wasn't. If he was grinding his teeth and clenching his fists in his pockets, it was only because . . .

Aw, fuck it. She was winning. Touching his plants, his stuff, picking a damn unripe squash. He couldn't let it go, even though he knew that was her plan all along.

He threw open the window, pushing his face close to the screen. "I'm calling the cops," he shouted.

"Oh, I wish you wouldn't," the redhead answered just as casual as you please. "I only want to have a civil conversation."

"Hell to the no, lady. I know what Gallagher means by *civil*, and it's *screw me six ways to Sunday* and then he'd expect me to thank him for it."

"As you can see, *Mr.* Gallagher isn't here."

"Just because you have breasts doesn't mean I'm more inclined to talk to you." Even if they were rather distracting when she was kneeling facing his window. From his higher vantage point, he could see down the gap between fabric and skin. Dark lace against very pale skin. A few freckles across her chest and cheeks. He briefly thought of his last email from D.

*Maybe we couldn't wait, and I unbutton and unzip your pants right there on your front porch.*

He couldn't think about the rest of that email and maintain his irritation, so he forced it out of his mind and focused on the offending party.

Her hair was a fashionable tangle of rich reddish waves. Her face was all made up with hues of pink, and the heels of her shoes sank into the mud next to his zucchini.

When she stood, wrinkling her freckled nose at him, he could see that she had long, lean legs, probably as pale and freckly as her chest, but black tights obscured them.

Which was good. This was one attraction he had no interest in pursuing. A Gallagher, for fuck's sake. Of course she was gorgeous. She probably paid a lot of money to be. Her family was rolling in it.

"I'm calling the cops," he threatened again.

"Don't you think they have better things to do?"

"Listen, lady—"

"All I want is ten minutes of your time, Mr. Trask. That's all. Much easier than getting the police involved."

She had a point and it wasn't like he was going to change his mind, but still, he knew the lay of the land. People with money managed to get what they wanted. People like him, people who just wanted to be left alone to work the land, to grow things and be at peace—those were the people trampled in the name of progress.

Ten minutes seemed innocuous, but it wouldn't be the end. They wouldn't accept his no. This was their third attempt at this point. Two from the sleaze in the suit, now an approach from these women.

Like he was going to change his mind just because of a change in tactics. Fat-ass chance. "Get off my property."

She continued to stare at him through the screen, and he didn't appreciate the scrutiny. It wasn't anything like the first Gallagher guy. That guy had been downright rude. A total asshole. Carter had trouble understanding why someone in business thought being a total dick was the way to win over someone, but he'd given up trying to understand people a long time ago.

"Maybe you could invite us in? Or we can talk out here if you'd be more comfortable."

Carter wanted to tell her no. He wanted to follow through on his threat to call the cops, but she was right. That was a waste of time for everyone involved. And worse, so much worse, she was still touching his plants.

There was something uncomfortably sexy in the way she let a finger trail over a leaf. Yeah, he'd go talk to them and get them out of here ASAP.

He stalked back outside to his porch, resisting the urge to go to the shed and find the most pointy, threatening gardening tool he had. Barely.

"I'm not selling. Period. I don't need to listen to anyone for ten minutes. My answer was, is, and always will be *no*. Especially to a Gallagher."

She moved to the bottom of his stairs, pleasant smile never leaving her face. "Please, call me Dinah. I understand that you've put a lot of work into this place." She gestured around them. "It's lovely."

"Yeah, and you guys want to make it into a parking lot."

"Not a parking lot. No, a farmers' market." She glanced back at the other redhead still standing near the entrance. Carter didn't understand the look, the slight slant of confusion to her eyebrows. The other redhead shrugged, the frown of worry never leaving her face.

"Just what did Craig Gallagher tell you?" the Dinah person asked, some of that easy pleasantness leaving her voice.

"I don't know what your game is, but you all work together, so why the hell don't you know what he told me?"

Another exchanged look between the two women. "We'd like to get your side of things. We want to make things beneficial for everyone."

Carter snorted. Yeah, he'd heard that line before. "We must have very different definitions of mutually beneficial. Rich people usually do."

She pursed her lips. "I think there's been some kind of misunderstanding."

"I heard all I need to hear. Your boss, or dad, or whoever, wants to buy me out and pave this place over for some kind of extra parking for Gallagher's Tap Room. Well, even if that wasn't the worst idea I'd ever heard, I'd still be saying no. This place is mine, and I'm not selling."

Let the rest of his family turn tail and leave, this Trask was standing his ground.

"Dinah, come on, let's head out. We'll reevaluate."

Dinah glanced behind her, then back at him, the frown line never leaving her forehead. Something wasn't right, not with the way the first guy had acted, not with the way these two were acting, but that wasn't his concern.

His only concern was to say no.

But Dinah Gallagher stepped forward, holding out a card. "Please, take this." She forced a smile, but it barely curved the edges of her pink tinted, full lips. "If you find you have ten minutes—that's all—I'm sure we can clear up this misunderstanding."

*Yeah, right.* But she took his hand, pressed the little business card to his palm, her pale skin with dark pink nails looking out of place against his tanned, dirty hands. When her fingers brushed his palm, the electric current of attraction didn't surprise him. But it did irritate him.

A Gallagher with a "misunderstanding." Yeah, not on his life.

"Don't come here again." His voice didn't sound nearly as forceful as he wanted it to.

She gave him a small, sad smile and a wave and walked back to her colleague. Together, they exited the yard, and he couldn't see them beyond the arches and rows of plants.

Which was good. He didn't want to see them, and he wouldn't ever again if he could help it.

# Chapter 2

When Dinah stepped inside her apartment at the end of the day, she hurled her bag across the living room. It landed with a satisfying thud against the couch.

She'd fumed all day, tried to magically transform anger into work, but all she could do was boil and pace and throw things.

Uncle Craig was setting her up for failure. He wasn't a dumb man, especially when it came to business. The only reason he'd riled up Trask was to sabotage her. They weren't planning on building a *parking lot*. They were planning on building a *farmers' market*. And yes, that might mean paving over the little farm this guy already had going, but what was going to be more lucrative for this area? Some loner farmer growing things in his yard, or a whole area devoted to people selling their local produce?

Telling Trask it was for a parking lot undermined everything they were really trying to do, and it was personal. She couldn't believe Craig had slipped up and picked the wrong words to win this guy over. Craig wanted her to fail. All because her dad had run off with his wife.

He hated her father *that* much. To take it out on her. To take it out on *Gallagher's*. As if she or their plans had anything to do with it. She hadn't told her father to sleep with Aunt Linda. Certainly hadn't condoned their running off together and leaving the rest of the family with the aftermath. Not that Mom had stuck around for the aftermath. She'd disappeared just as Dad had. Leaving Dinah with angry, hurting family members.

Why on earth was Craig punishing *her*? She'd never particularly cared for her uncle. He was cold and ruthless—even his own daughter thought so—but still . . . Gallagher's was a family affair.

And he wanted her out. It was the only explanation for telling Trask a parking lot was in the plans. That *wasn't* the plan.

She screamed in frustration. Then she flopped onto her couch. She knew life wasn't fair, that was a given, but there had to be some way she could fix this. Why couldn't she find the fix?

*My answer was, is, and always will be no.*

"We'll see about that, mister." Everyone had a point to fold, a concession to make with the right stakes. A guy like him had to see that growing things didn't belong in the middle of city traffic and bustle. A guy like him had to see that the money they would offer could build him something bigger and better elsewhere.

She'd convince him. She'd find that concession, that point to fold, and she'd show Uncle Craig where he could shove his sabotage.

She flipped open her laptop, ready to do some more research on Carter Trask. But her email was up, her last email with C.

He'd written, *I'd like to think we'd be the kind of people who wouldn't get tired of each other. We could eat together, have sex, read, work, hand-in-hand, and never give up, never walk away. I'd like to think we could be those people, even if it's just a fantasy.*

He wrote like poetry. Sure, they traded elaborate sexual fantasies, but he ended each email or exchange with something kind and sweet. Something romantic, the further along this thing went. Fantasy, yes, that's exactly what they had.

But, in the past eight months, though she still only knew the bare minimum about the details of his life, she felt like she knew him. Or at least the email version of him. She didn't know if that was real, but she'd given him pieces of herself, her real self.

It was probably really warped, but he was comfort—without having to risk . . . well, anything. He couldn't make her feel useless, or break her heart. He could, at most, disappear, and that would suck, but she wouldn't lose anything except some invisible man on the other side of the keyboard.

She frowned at the thought of him disappearing. What would she do then when she was feeling restless and upset? Emailing with anyone else would seem wrong. As for going out and having some real sex, as Kayla had suggested, oddly enough the idea didn't appeal. Not with C in her inbox.

"Oh, Dinah, you are one royal screwball," she muttered to herself.

But this—C—he was all fantasy, so what did it matter how screwed up she was? Over life. Over this unorthodox emailing relationship thing. In their fantasy, it *didn't* matter, and right now she needed it not to.

She hit reply.

*What would you do if I came to your place in one of those trench coats and high heels, just like out of a movie. You invite me inside, I drop the jacket, and say, "I want you to fuck me."*

She stared at the words. It was the beauty of this situation. She could say all the things she was scared to say in real life. She'd never been able to bring herself to say *fuck* during sex before. Or *cock* or to beg for something harder or rougher. Anytime she had the inclination, embarrassment and fear of rejection had flooded her.

But here, with nothing but a computer screen glaring back at her, she could put all those fantasies into words. She was in charge and powerful and could ask—and get—whatever she wanted.

She hit send because she needed that right now, when everything felt completely out of her control. She needed to feel like something could go right, and if it meant a little fictional sex, well so be it. There were a lot worse ways to be a total wacko.

After only a few minutes, her email dinged. *I'd tell you to get in the bedroom and sit on the edge of my bed.*

Hallelujah. She switched over to the instant messaging program they'd been using lately, and C continued.

*I'd take my time following you. I like to watch you walk. I'd even guess something was wrong, but you don't want to talk about it, do you?*

Talk? No. The only words she wanted were dirty ones. In fact, that's exactly what she'd write.

She liked a lot of things about C. The descriptive way he wrote, the sweetness he could infuse into the dirtiest of scenarios, but mostly she liked that he was an incredibly fast typist because his responses didn't take long.

*I didn't think so. So, I let you sit down, and then I'd tell you to take off your coat. And your shirt. And your skirt. Slip off your heels and your tights.*

He knew what she'd be wearing; they'd talked about it often enough. Workday meant skirt and heels. Weekends meant jeans and tennis shoes. Saturday nights meant lingerie she'd made up at first, then bought . . . just because.

This *was* pathetic, wasn't it?

But she kept reading, because pathetic or not, his words were hot and she wanted to get off on them. The fantasy. Sex without worrying about anything. Not the other person. Not herself.

*Tell me what your underwear looks like. In great detail.*

Oh, she had some great detail for him. *Today, it's all black lace. My underwear is completely sheer, except for the black thread polka dots. My bra is the same. You can see my nipples. They're already hard, just watching you watching me. I spread my legs, because that's exactly where I want you.*

*Because you want to be fucked?*

*Yes. Hard. Nothing nice about it.*

*I can do that. First, I'd tell you to stand up. An order, like a teacher instructing a student. You'd like that, wouldn't you? If I told you exactly what I wanted you to do.*

*I'd do whatever you want.*

*I'd tell you to bend over the bed, and I'd make you wait, your ass in the air, so I could really appreciate your entire backside. So I could think about all the things I'm going to do to you. So I could torture myself while I'm torturing you, because you don't know what to expect.*

Dinah's breath went heavy. Damn, he was so good at this. She might not know what he looked like, but she could see it all. Feel it all. Unfolding in front of her like a dream.

*And then I'd smack my palm against your ass.*

She groaned into the silence of her apartment. She'd never given much thought to spanking, but just the idea, the fantasy of it, had her rolling her tights off, pulling off her shirt. Instead of shimmying out of her skirt, she just inched it up around her waist.

She was wet. Her nipples *were* hard, and as much as she wished for this to be real, it was real enough.

*You'd be so wet. I'd just slide my finger over the outside of your panties and I could feel it. How much you want me. And then, I think you'd beg.*

*I would. I'd beg. I'd beg you to fuck me. Hard and rough with that big cock. I'd say I'd do anything for it.*

It always amazed her, the words she wrote. Such half-finished fantasies she never allowed herself in reality. But here? Here she could beg and plead for whatever she wanted.

*Anything. That's a lot of power to hand over to someone. I'd slide your panties down your legs, slowly, making sure every inch of each hand was always touching your skin. You'd feel each callus, each rough bump and scrape along those smooth, pale legs of yours. Once I got the panties to your ankles, I'd kiss my way back up. Calf, the back of your knee, thigh. What do you want, baby? My mouth or my cock?*

*Cock. Please. Hurry.* Because she'd cheated a little and already slid her finger across her sex, sliding it back and forth, enjoying those first few jolts of utter arousal. But now she wanted more than jolts. She wanted everything.

*I'd settle the head of my cock right at your pussy, but I'd make you wait. I'm not pushing inside until you beg.*

*Please. Please. I need you inside me.* Which was frighteningly true, but she'd deal with that fear of need some other time.

*I'd thrust, as deep as I can go, and I'd settle myself right there until you begged again.*

It wasn't hard to pretend. She used her fingers exactly as he said he'd use his cock. When she wasn't typing, she circled her nipples with her fingertips. The excitement grew, her breathing growing heavier with each *please fuck me harder* she tapped out.

*Are you pretending your fingers are my cock, sliding into you? Fast and hard, just what you asked for.*

*Yes, yes. I'm going to come. Fucking my fingers. Thinking of you.*

*Make yourself come, baby. Pretend it's me making you come.*

It didn't take much more. She was an expert on getting herself off at this point. The wave of pleasure, release from all that manic tension, swept through her. As the climax fizzled out, she all but melted on the couch.

Relaxed. Satisfied. Mostly, anyway.

*And then I'd make you crawl under the covers, and I'd get you a glass of wine, and you'd tell me about your day.*

Why wasn't this real?

At first, she'd never had those thoughts. Of course, at first it was just sexmailing. Something about the last few weeks had morphed it into . . . more. Like the glass of wine and talking about what's wrong—even if she didn't respond, the offer was there.

She held her breath and counted to ten. She was not going to suggest they meet because that would ruin everything. What they'd just done was the only thing she wanted.

So, why didn't she feel better? Sure, a little satisfied, but mainly she was just as angry at Craig as she had been, and she felt just as powerless. Just as restless and frustrated.

*Good night, C. Thanks.* She hit send and rested her head back on the couch, looking up at the plain apartment ceiling. Nothing was going the way she'd planned. Work. Love life. At twenty-seven she was supposed to be farther along.

So why was she stuck?

Well, screw being stuck. She needed to grab the reins of her spiraling-off-course life.

She poked around on the Internet for a while, idly flipping through Tumblr. Looking for inspiration, a spark of an idea. She followed a few fashion people, a few foodies, and then C's page.

She stopped at his latest post, felt a weird wave of unease settle over her.

The image of the front yard of Front Yard Farm had stuck with her all day. The arches, the rows of plants. The redbrick pathways. It was all so damn familiar, and not because it was situated next to Gallagher's Tap Room. She never went that way. She'd never stopped to ponder Front Yard Farm.

But this picture . . . it was Front Yard Farm. It was. What were the chances . . .

No. Impossible. She was jumping to conclusions. Just because he uploaded the photo instead of reblogging it from another site, just because the caption read *my little slice of heaven*, did not mean . . .

There was no way. No chance. She clicked on his main page and scrolled through his pictures, photos she'd mooned over without thinking about it. Pictures she hadn't placed. Captions she hadn't fit together into a puzzle.

C worked with his hands, worked with the land. He talked about plants. And his father had been a farmer. He'd said that in one of his emails. *When I was a kid on my dad's farm . . .*

But how could this be? How was it possible that she'd started emailing with a guy who . . .

"Oh my God." It couldn't be, but this . . . this all worked together as irrefutable proof. She'd been sexmailing Carter Trask.

"Well, fuck."

\*  \*  \*

The pounding on his door was a surprise. Carter glanced down at his half-eaten dinner, thought idly of ignoring the door, but the pounding kept reverberating through the century-old house.

"All right. All right," he grumbled. He flipped on the porch light and glanced out the peephole. "Jesus Christ. Don't you people ever give up?"

Wrenching open the door, he scowled down at Dinah Gallagher. She was dressed the same as this afternoon, sans tights and heels. Instead she had on bright purple sneakers that did not match her office-ready outfit or bright yellow jacket at all.

"This is you!"

Carter squinted at the phone screen being shoved into his face. It was his Tumblr page. "Yeah. So?"

"*You! You're* the one writing me sex-mails!"

"What the hell is a sex-mail?" Oh. Wait. No. She couldn't be . . . He felt a little sick to his stomach. This was some kind of prank.

"You! You!"

Well, if her panic was any indication, no prank. "Calm down." He was talking more to himself than to her. If what she was saying meant . . . somehow . . . he'd been trading dirty emails with a Gallagher for *eight months.* Oh, not okay. So completely not okay.

"My career depends on the grumpy farmer I've been writing sex-mails to." She flung her arms into the air, pacing the tiny box of his stoop.

"Christ, stop yelling *sex-mail.* My eighty-year-old neighbor will hear you and chew me out."

"I just . . . You are . . ." She was waving her phone around and Mrs. Washington's porch light flipped on, so against his better judgment, Carter pulled her inside.

"Calm down," he said, this time to her. Very much to her.

Dinah Gallagher. D. His mind instantly went to their email exchange. The one that had made him postpone dinner until well past his normal eating time.

Because she'd wanted him to fuck her.

*Metaphorically. Fictionally. Not . . . now.*

Right?

He should be pushing her *out* the door, not leading her through it. "Is this some joke? Some elaborate scheme?"

She fisted her hands on her hips. "Are you high? We've been doing this for almost a year!"

Wow. That sounded pathetic. But it also made him think about all the things they'd written to each other. All the ways he'd fictionally fucked her. This gorgeous woman standing in his living room.

Gallagher. She was a Gallagher. She wanted to buy the last piece of himself he had left. Beautiful or not—D or not—this could not change anything.

*Please fuck me harder. Pound that big cock into me.* Hello, unwelcome erection. But seriously, how was he supposed to just not remember those words she'd typed him not that long ago?

Touching herself. His gaze drifted to the hem of her skirt. She hadn't changed out of the outfit she'd been wearing this morning, so she was still wearing what she'd had on as she'd gotten herself off over his words. Was she wearing the see-through underwear she'd described to him? Because he'd seen a hint of black lace this morning and . . .

His dick was so hard it hurt, and when he forced himself to look back up at her, she was staring, not at his face, but at his very obvious erection.

"Sorry, he's not as business-minded as me," Carter managed.

She inhaled sharply, her cheeks tinging pink. "I'm not sure my lady parts are as business-minded as I am, either." She sounded a little breathless, and that was enough to think, remember, imagine.

*I'm going to come. Fucking my fingers. Thinking of you.*

"You should go." His voice was rusty, unsteady, and anything but sure.

"Yes, yes I should." She nodded, turned away, but her steps were slow. He wanted to stop her.

*No.*

"What if . . ." She trailed off, her what-if hanging in the air and his dick hanging on every word. No. No what-ifs. There could be no what-ifs. Maybe she was the fantasy he'd spent way too much online time with, but that didn't mean anything said on a computer was real, honest.

"What if I said I wanted you to fuck me. Like, for real." She stuttered a little over the word *fuck.* And she kept her back to him.

But she didn't leave or laugh or take it back. She just stood there. Waiting.

And he stood there not knowing how to answer, because the truth was if he stripped away her name and her job, he very much wanted to fuck her, and it was hard to think about her name and her job when she was in his living room saying *fuck*.

"What if . . ." She turned, slowly, her shoulders straightening, her gaze zeroing in on his. "We . . . pretended the real us didn't exist. Just this once. And lived out the fantasy us. Just this once."

No, no, no. Bad idea. Terrible idea. She could even be playing him. She wanted his land, he knew that.

But the no in his mind didn't form on his lips.

# Chapter 3

It was a weird moment, both of them standing in the middle of his cozy, cluttered little house staring at each other. Her proposition hung in the air.

It was a crazy proposition. Wrong and crazy and so out of character and . . . yes, that was why she'd made it. There was power in stepping outside yourself. Power in fantasy.

She wanted some damn power.

"Just . . . just this once?"

"C and D." Her voice was all sultry and smooth, and though her insides jittered, she was doing a pretty good job of seeming like the kind of woman who propositioned men with one-night stands any old time.

"And tomorrow when we're back to being on opposites sides of the coin?"

"That's Carter and Dinah. Trask and Gallagher. This is . . ." She was going to say *just us*, because this felt more real than the person she was at Gallagher's, but that was probably her own weird baggage.

"You really think that's possible?"

"Maybe. Maybe not. I'm having a hard time caring right now."

"It seemed pretty important to you this morning."

"That was before I knew I was being set up for failure." She probably shouldn't have said that, but it was true. This morning she'd had a strength of purpose. Now . . . "So, what's your answer?"

He paused, a silence that seemed to stretch out endlessly. But it wasn't a no, so she waited. And maybe she was silently willing him to *please* agree. She wanted sex. Real sex. With him. To feel like something . . . something could go her way. Just because she wanted it to. Because she'd asked for it.

"My bedroom is the second door on the right."

Oh God. They were going to do this. She was going to walk to his bedroom and he was going to fuck her. This man she only knew from emails and a brief interaction this morning. She had all the earmarks of being too stupid to live, but she walked down the hallway anyway.

He watched her, just as he'd said he would. Even with her heart pounding in her ears, she put a little swing to her step. Because this was supposed to be fun. Fantasy. She was damn well going to enjoy herself.

Ignoring nerves, refusing to accept them, she sauntered her way over to his unmade bed. She sat on the rumpled black comforter, just like the email had instructed her to. But she couldn't quite bring herself to remove any clothing.

Yet. She would. She so would.

He stepped into the room, closing the door behind him. She didn't fidget. She wouldn't. Instead, she looked up at him and smiled. "I hope you have condoms."

"Yes."

"Good." That was good. She might be crazy, but she wasn't stupid. She hoped.

But he stood there, feet away from her, arms crossed over his chest, frowning. It was an oddly good look for him. Broody and intense over mean or standoffish.

"Problem?" she asked, a lightness in her voice she wanted desperately to feel. Fake it till you make it.

"We've never even kissed."

She blinked. That hadn't been what she'd expected. But, what had she expected? She had no idea. But she kept the smile in place. "So kiss me, C."

He stepped toward her, brow furrowed, wavy hair a little unruly and his beard somewhat neatly cropped. Her breath hitched a little in her chest because she was sitting on his bed and he was hovering above her, all tense and serious and yum.

Then he touched the tip of his index finger to her cheek, drew it across what she assumed was the pattern of freckles there. He'd said in his email he had a thing for freckles.

Well, lucky him.

When his head bent, mouth bridging the distance to hers, she had to fight the need to fidget. Or move. Or grab him by the neck and kiss him hard. Maybe later. Right now, she kind of liked the wild anticipation in her racing heart and unsteady breath.

His lips barely brushed hers, and that excitement doubled, tripled. The finger on her cheek became his whole hand, cupping her face, pulling her closer, his mouth pressing to hers. Sinking deeper and deeper until his tongue traced her bottom lip, and she opened her mouth to return the favor.

It wasn't the kind of kiss she'd expected. This wasn't quick or heated or even weird, it was lazy exploration. It was *amazing*. The rasp of his beard against her chin, his rough hands traveling down her neck.

Every word that had been amazing and beautiful still managed to pale in comparison to the reality of his mouth on hers.

He pulled back, his expression unreadable. Of course, the erection making itself a very obvious bump under his jeans was readable. *Very* readable. He might be uncertain, but he wasn't unaffected.

"Take off your coat."

She swallowed, but got that thing off as fast as she possibly could. If the kiss was *that* good. Just one kiss. Oh man, the rest might melt her from the inside out.

"You really did have a shit day, huh?" he asked, forehead still not smoothing out.

"The shittiest."

"And this is your answer?"

"An orgasm I don't have to give myself is a hell of an answer."

He leaned closer, his mouth brushing against her ear. "Then I'll make sure you get two, D."

It helped to use the poorly coded nicknames. She didn't think about the man who'd threatened to call the cops on her. She thought about the man who might make her beg for things she'd never had the courage to beg for before.

"The rest," he instructed.

She unbuttoned her blouse, determined to be sexy and sure. She was a smart, mature twenty-something who was going to enjoy some casual, consensual sex. If it was a little out of character, good. She'd gotten a whole lot of nothing for staying in character.

So, she shimmied out of her skirt and gave him her best come-hither look. "Your turn."

Slowly, he pulled the T-shirt up and over his head, then undid his belt, the button to his jeans, the zipper.

Dinah swallowed. Funny, she thought she'd want to bolt, but what she really wanted to do was help him out of his clothes. Touch every expanse of tanned skin over rangy muscles he exposed.

He took a step closer so their knees touched. He rested his hands on her thighs, hot and rough. "You're . . . The picture I had in my head falls short of you in reality."

Oh God. Hot. Sweet. Amazing kisser. This *was* a fantasy. It couldn't possibly be real. "You hold up pretty well yourself."

He leaned in for a kiss, and this one wasn't languid or exploratory. It was tongue and teeth and need. His hands moved up her thighs, to her hips, her back. He unsnapped her bra and pulled it off. And then his mouth was on her neck, her chest, openmouthed kisses across her breasts.

She ran her hands over his abdomen, the slight dip of muscles, beyond the hem of his boxers to hot, hard male.

Normally she'd be all for a lot more foreplay, but the situation, the words of the email bouncing around her head—she was dying for this to be more. Dying to be *fucked.*

She was going to beg, because for some reason that made the need sharper, deeper, more everything.

Heart in her throat, nerves battling courage, frustration battling fear, she gave him a nudge so she had room. She slid her panties off and turned on the bed so she could bend over it like they'd laid out in their exchange from earlier. "Now, please, fuck me."

He cleared his throat, a noise akin to uncertainty, so she grinned over her shoulder at him. She liked this feeling of power, like maybe she surprised him. Dependable, hardworking Dinah never surprised anyone.

But he merely stepped closer so she could feel his presence, his body heat, and then he caressed a hand over the curve of her ass. Oh God, was he going to spank her? This was some demented version of role play, wasn't it? Acting out all they'd written to each other.

She didn't plan to speak, to draw attention to it, but as his hand caressed, a *please* escaped her mouth, said in a moan.

His hand drew away, then she felt the slight tap of his palm against her skin. So light it didn't even jolt let alone hurt, but somehow sent shock waves of lust through her.

"I need you inside me. Now. Get a condom, please. Please."

Out of her peripheral vision she saw him rummage around in a drawer, pulling out a square packet and ripping it open. He returned to his position behind her.

She watched over her shoulder as he rolled the condom on. Thick and hard, he was going to do exactly as she asked. No fingers, no vague sense of missing out on something by doing it herself. He was going to pound her into orgasm, and she was going to return the favor.

He settled behind her, one big hand gripping her hip. She felt him nudge, slowly, but it didn't take much. She was so wet and ready for this. After all this time, all those words, finally real.

She moaned as he filled her completely, buried deep inside, his hips flush with her ass. Oh, this was so much better than do-it-yourself.

"You feel so good," he murmured. "So damn good. Are you going to keep begging, just like we did before?"

"Whatever you want, remember?"

"Then beg. I love it when you beg."

So she did. She begged and pleaded with each thrust, egging him on with every please, every request for harder or more. She gripped the comforter, pressed her forehead into the mattress.

It didn't take long for the orgasm to build, swell. Not when his hands gripped her hips hard enough to leave marks and his cock hit every right spot as it pushed deep.

"Yeah, that's it, baby. Come on my cock. I need it. I need you to come. Please. Please."

It was his *please* that sent her over the edge to pulsing, exhausting, *amazing* orgasm.

Still fully sheathed inside her, he rubbed a hand up and down her spine and she slowly let go of the covers, flexing her fingers.

"That was one," he said on a not-so-steady breath, withdrawing from her. "Now, I think for two you should do some of the work." He sat on the bed now, scooted himself back to the headboard, then motioned for her to get on top.

She straddled his lap, already desperate to have him inside her again. So she guided him inside, pressed her breasts to his chest. "Remember the time we were like this and I tied you up?" Probably weird to call it remembering when it had just been words, but oh well.

"Vividly."

She took his hands in hers, lifted them until they rested straight out on either side against the headboard. "So let's pretend."

His eyes were dark, intense, and it didn't feel like having sex with a stranger, and that was probably the worst thing she could feel. But she'd be damned if she was going to care about that right now.

Dinah—D—whoever—was everything he'd ever imagined she would be. Possibly more. It was intimidating, really. Probably the only thing that kept his head together, because holy hell this was amazing.

She held his arms back against the headboard. Her breasts brushed against his chest and her mouth closed over his shoulder as she bit lightly.

He groaned, his head falling back and hitting the wall. He didn't care.

"Mm. You like that?"

"I think I've been very clear on the subject."

She lifted herself slowly, then sank back down so he was buried completely. She was so tight, so warm.

"I did promise you two orgasms, though, so tread lightly."

She grinned. Wicked and playful. Her lipstick was mostly smudged off, her hair tousled, her cheeks pink. Yeah, he'd promised her two, she was damn well going to get two.

He took his hands from hers and she pouted. "I thought you were tied up."

"I need my hands for this, just once." He smoothed his hands over her thighs, because he couldn't stop himself from soaking up the smoothness of her skin. She was so soft, and it was like comfort.

He didn't want thoughts like that right now, so his hands tightened at her hips, holding her steady so he could push deeper into her. Her head rolled back on a sigh, pushing her breasts into his face, so he took the opportunity to draw a nipple into his mouth, teasing it with his tongue, until she was the one setting the pace, riding him. Fast, hard.

She clutched his shoulders, nails digging into the skin. The prick of pressure sending him closer and closer to an edge he was just barely fighting off.

"Yes, oh, right there."

He couldn't get enough of the reverent way she said *oh*, the delicate sighs, the deep throaty moans. He hadn't been lying when he'd said she was even better than his imagination. She was. Every freckle, every smile, every inch of pale, soft skin.

"Yes. Yes. Again." She rode him faster, at breakneck speed he could barely keep up with. But the way she chanted *yes* and *this*, he had a feeling she was close again, so he just held on for the ride.

She pushed deep against him, her nails digging even harder into his shoulders, a sound somewhere between a moan and a sigh.

"Oh, wow, that's good," she whispered in his ear. Then she bit his earlobe and he was a goner.

Release rumbled through him, heavy and powerful. Buried deep inside her, her breath quick and heavy against his neck, he already regretted that she'd have to leave. That this was *just once.*

Because it was the pretend world brought to life, and it was going to be a bitch to go back to only pretend.

After a few minutes she rolled off him. She gave him a smile, shy almost. He wanted to smile back, kiss her, say things could be different.

But he didn't lie to people. Or tiptoe around the truth. He'd learned that was a shit end of the stick to be on.

She slid off the bed, already retrieving her underwear. So he got up too and went to the bathroom and cleaned himself up.

The silence was weird, but he didn't know how to fix that or even if he should. When he returned to the room she was stepping into her skirt.

"That was . . ." She trailed off as she pulled the skirt back up over her hips, zipped it up. "Just right," she finished, her voice a little soft. He couldn't see her face to try to read her expression.

"Yeah." Lame, but what was he supposed to do? Talk to her? About the reality of the situation? Talk to her and pretend? It didn't seem right.

But he did want her to stay, to talk, just like their emails. Because he was an idiot, apparently, and forgetting all about her last name.

"Thanks, C." Now fully dressed, she brushed a kiss across his mouth and then she was walking out his bedroom door. As it should be. As it only *could* be.

# Chapter 4

Dinah woke up the next morning sore in places she never would have dreamed. She should feel mortified. Horrified. Everything about her behavior last night should be an absolute embarrassment.

She was really struggling to find that horror or self-disgust. But she was just a little too pleased with herself. She had done something she had only ever dreamed of doing. Maybe it was wrong, and maybe she would suffer some consequences in the future, but for now, having to face the reality of her situation with Uncle Craig, she might as well enjoy the memories of last night.

She drove to Gallagher's feeling more philosophical than she had in a while. It was a quick drive from her apartment to the restaurant.

Much had changed in the two decades she could remember. Some good, some bad. The city certainly wasn't the same place it had been when her great-great-grandparents had started Gallagher's, but regardless of the way the city had changed around it, she *loved* the place. It was her legacy, and even if that legacy didn't match the city as well as it used to, that didn't mean she could give up on something she believed in so passionately.

She parked in the employee lot around the back of the brick building. Brick columns ran up the three stories, covered in a green ivy she'd always assumed was the inspiration for the street name that connected with Gallagher Street. The windows on each level were trimmed in black in the back, pretty white cornices in the front. It was sandwiched by other old brick buildings, all with a variety of styles of windows and embellishments.

She loved the *history* of it all, that her ancestors had walked all over this ground, put their stamp on that building, and now she got to honor their work and add her own flare.

It was a good reminder after last night. She still couldn't bring herself to *regret*, but in the face of her life's work, she had to remember why Carter Trask couldn't be anything more than a one-night liability.

Uncle Craig's sleek BMW was nowhere to be seen in the lot. She was slightly relieved, since she hadn't figured out exactly what her plan of attack was going to be. She would need Kayla's help. With any luck, Kayla had thought of something last night. Assuming she had been alone and not diving into any fantasies brought to life, as Dinah had been.

Again Dinah waited for the shame to swamp her. Again, it didn't appear. She smiled instead.

She walked into the back and up the stairs to the offices on the second floor. The restaurant and bar wouldn't come to life until later, but she'd always loved this time of day. When the first floor was quiet, and the second floor pulsed with *business*.

"I guess you didn't take to heart my lecture about being on time."

Dinah came to a complete stop at her grandmother's voice. Wide-eyed and startled, she glanced up to find Grandmother standing ominously at the end of the hallway.

Lucille Dinah Gallagher was an imposing figure even in her early eighties. Though she had married at twenty, she had insisted on keeping the Gallagher name and giving it to her children in a generation where that was frowned upon. The oldest Gallagher of her generation, though she had stepped aside for her son thirty-five years ago, she had remained a constant figure at Gallagher's Tap Room.

A constant looming, scary figure. Dinah was both 100 percent intimidated by her and 100 percent in awe of her. She admired her grandmother fiercely, and she loved her as much as Grandmother allowed.

That was the tricky part. "I thought you were in Chicago." Dinah beamed at her in a way that had Grandmother narrowing her eyes.

"You'd certainly like it if I were in Chicago. Slinking in here late."

"Grandmother," Dinah admonished. "I'm five minutes early."

The older woman scowled in return. "Five minutes early is ten minutes late." Grandmother gave her a quick flick of a glance that amounted to a once-over. "Kayla told me you talked to Trask yesterday. I assume it was unsuccessful?"

Dinah tried to keep her smile in place. She had always assumed

Grandmother gave her a hard time because it was the only way she knew how to express her love. At least, Dinah really hoped that was the case.

But when it came to business, Grandmother was *all* Gallagher, and *zero* grandmother. So much so, Dinah hesitated spouting off about Craig trying to sabotage her. With her luck, Grandmother would just tell her that if she wanted to be DOO, she'd have to outmaneuver him.

So, rather than let Grandmother think she was weak or whining, Dinah decided to keep the challenge to herself. That's all it was, after all. A challenge. That's how Grandmother would view it.

Dinah wasn't sure she completely wanted to be like her grandmother, but she *mostly* wanted to be like her. She just . . . never quite knew how.

It was amazing how much that kept coming up; that she didn't know how to be the things she wanted to be. With Grandmother. With Gallagher. Hell, even with . . . Carter. C.

"Dinah."

She met her grandmother's shrewd gaze and tried to smile. "Mr. Trask has a very significant emotional connection to his land, and it seems he's been a little misinformed about our purpose in wanting to buy it. But I have no doubt I'll convince him."

"How soon?"

Dina's weak smile faltered, but she refused to break eye contact. She knew how easy it was for Grandmother to spot weakness.

"I'm not sure, but I have no doubt I'll be successful. I just might need some time in order to convince him."

"I want his agreement by the end of October, and all papers signed by the end of the year."

"And if I fail?" Dinah asked, not because she thought she would fail but because she sincerely wondered what Grandmother's plans were if Dinah didn't do exactly what Grandmother had asked. Dinah had always lived up to Grandmother's expectations, though sometimes by the skin of her teeth. She wouldn't let her down now.

But she was a little curious what failure would look like.

"You're a Gallagher, Dinah. Failure is not an option." With that, Grandmother stepped into Craig's office and the door closed behind her with an audible click.

"Psst."

Dinah looked over to where Kayla was sticking her head out of her office door. "Is it safe?"

"I don't think it's ever safe."

Kayla smiled. "True enough."

"Have you been hiding from her the whole time?"

"You know how much that woman scares me," Kayla answered with an exaggerated shudder as Dinah stepped into Kayla's sunshiny little office.

Dinah slipped her arm around Kayla's shoulders. "She's your grandmother."

"She's Lucille Gallagher. I'm under no illusions that our relationship means anything to her. You being the oldest lends you some leeway, but me? The daughter of the second Gallagher? It's like being . . . I don't know, those grapes at the bottom of the bag that are all shriveled up and only the most desperate people eat."

"Kayla, you're crazy. And I love you. We have got to figure this out. What's your schedule today?"

Dinah took a seat across from Kayla's desk and they went over Kayla's day as sustainability manager. She had some meetings to attend, and Dinah had a few things that she would have to do for Uncle Craig in the morning, but in the afternoon they could focus on the Trask problem together.

Right now, she wasn't quite sure she trusted herself to focus on it alone. Not with Grandmother's looming *Gallaghers don't fail* edict hanging over her head.

"I don't think anything is going to matter to that man. Not after the way he talked to us. This might be—"

"Everyone has a point to fold," Dinah said forcefully. "Everyone has a straw that will break their back. We just have to find it." And she had to keep C and Carter as two different people in her mind.

"What if he's sitting in his little—adorable, by the way—house thinking the same thing? That there's some way to break us from being Gallagher's bitches? That all he has to do is find a weakness?"

Dinah felt the uncomfortable truth of that statement settle in her gut. Though she hadn't known it at the time, she *had* gotten to know at least the Internet version of Carter Trask. Which seemed to be pretty damn close to the real him. He talked about land like it was his . . . Not even like it was his girlfriend or his wife, but like it was his god. His religion. What were the chances she'd get through to a man who viewed farming as a calling?

"You're worried," Kayla accused.

"No. I'm thinking. Gallagher's has been here for over a century. We're not going anywhere. He's got nothing on our century."

"But we're not going anywhere even if we don't get his land. It's not like we fail if we don't get that land."

"It'll be *my* failure. And, as Grandmother so lovingly reminded me, Gallaghers don't fail."

"I think there are a lot of ways to fail, and not all of them have to do with this business."

Dinah was sure Kayla felt that, but her cousin didn't have the same kind of pressure on her, and she didn't have the same kind of connection. Kayla was more interested in her sustainability and green initiatives than she was in the integrity and the history of Gallagher's. As one of the seconds, it hadn't been poured into her like blood.

Gallagher's was Dinah's own religion to compare to Carter's. The thing she worshipped and breathed and believed and *needed*.

And hers was bigger, deeper, and more damn important. So she wasn't going to lose. No way in hell.

Carter cut himself on a jagged corner of brick edging, for the third time that morning. He kept meaning to stop and fix it, but then would get completely distracted by his squash.

He was *never* distracted at work. His work was everything. His life, his soul, his promise. But last night had left him . . .

It had been a long time since he'd been this mixed up. Since anything had reached through and touched him as deeply as the land touched him.

Which was moronic. Everything with D—*Dinah Gallagher*—had been emails and instant messages. It had been fake. Like reading a book or watching a movie. Even though he'd poured his own self into it, the exchanges didn't require anything of him. He could be moved, or not moved. It was all about *him*.

But she was real, and she had come to him last night. Now he had to deal with how that affected him and . . .

Gallagher. Her name was like a fucking cancer. He couldn't get it out of his head, not her name, not last night. Just across the way, Gallagher's Tap Room stood in all its ivy-covered brick, century-old glory, and he sat here in this barely surviving century-old house. Barely . . . At best he was barely holding on to his legacy. At best, barely scraping by.

He sat back on his haunches and looked at the house his grandmother had lived in her whole life until she'd been moved into the nursing home. Her family's restaurant had been only two blocks away, though it had been demolished a few years ago to make way for a trendy new apartment complex.

She'd always kept a garden here, mostly herbs that she would harvest and use in the kitchen. He remembered her puttering in the back, and he could perfectly picture the way her face would light up when someone paid their compliments to the chef.

When she'd been diagnosed with Alzheimer's, there had been no one in the family willing to take over the restaurant, willing to fight for it. He was no chef, no restaurateur, and so it had gone.

Just like the farm he'd grown up on, west of St. Louis. Just like his uncle's farm where Carter had worked while Grandma had worked the restaurant. The city had crumbled, and farms had been sold to build up suburbia.

Carter had never been on the right side of history. Not. Ever.

Dinah Gallagher could be a fantasy, but she could not have this little piece of him. This *last* piece of who he was and what he'd come from.

She did not get to take this over and turn it into Gallagher's, no matter *what*. He had built this *farm* from his grandmother's poorly kept yard. He'd cultivated this soil and grown these plants in *this* place as a testament to all that he had in him.

One night of insanely hot and really, really, really ill-advised sex was not going to change the course of his life. He wouldn't allow it. As much as he'd been tempted to ask Dinah to stay, or to ask her for more, he couldn't give in to that. Because it didn't matter what was beneath all the layers of fantasy they'd written to each other; it didn't matter if seeds of truth existed.

Their *reality* was that she wanted the land he had fought for. Fought to keep and build and cultivate.

No, last night had to be a one-time mistake. Something he could never, ever return to.

So, it was time to stop looking over in the direction of Gallagher's and focus on the day ahead. He had fall vegetables to harvest for tomorrow morning's farmers' market, and then this afternoon he was giving a brief tour to a class from a local charter school.

That'd be good. Getting out of his head. Talking to kids who were patently amazed when he pulled a carrot out of the ground.

He focused on that as he worked harvesting the squash and the beans. He practiced the little pseudo-script he had for these visits as he washed and packaged the produce, and he most certainly didn't think of Dinah Gallagher.

Until he heard the unmistakable clip-clop of heels on the sidewalk outside his haven. Yesterday he might not have thought anything of it. People came and went in the neighborhood all day long. But the hairs on the back of his neck stood on end, and he *knew* she was back.

With the speed of a hero facing down the villain in an old movie, Carter stood and turned to face the entrance gate.

Dinah stood at the chain-link gate looking as she had yesterday afternoon—not as she had last night. She was all polish and color and a sleek sort of sophistication that made him want to itch, instead of the slightly disheveled, wounded woman who'd shown up at his door and shoved her phone in his face.

He always marveled at people who could be two things, because he'd never had any luck at that. At best he could sport a pissed-off façade, but that wasn't much different than his soul, truth be told.

"Mr. Trask," she greeted, all businesswoman coolness.

"Ms. Gallagher." He made sure to say her last name in the same tone he might say *fucking damn it*. Because though his brain was nothing but a string of curse words, his body was remembering other things.

The way those legs—clad today in what looked like some kind of lace tights—had wrapped around him, the sweet, wet slide of his cock straight into—

"You have to leave." She had to get the hell out. He trusted his brain to override his dick, but only just. He didn't want to chance it.

"I only wanted to clear up a misunderstanding between you and my uncle."

"Your uncle? Oh, the piece of shit spouting on about parking lots? I don't think that was a misunderstanding."

"It *was*," Dinah insisted, shoving a piece of paper at him. "If you'd look at our actual plans, you'd see how wrong—"

Carter scowled at it and shoved it back at her. "I do not care what your plans are. Parking lot. Homeless shelter. Vatican Jr. This land is mine and I ain't selling."

She pursed her lips. Lips he'd kissed, licked, bitten. Lips he wanted to sink into again.

*No. No, you don't.*

She pressed the piece of paper, what looked like some kind of sketch, back into his hands. "Keep it."

"No." He tried to hand it back to her, but she crossed her arms over her chest and tucked her hands underneath.

He didn't think about yanking her hands free, or nuzzling his mouth at the scoop of her shirt's neckline. Not at all.

"I'm not taking it back."

Carter shrugged, crumpled the piece of paper into a little ball, and tossed it at her feet. Being an asshole was his only fight against this stupid lust-fog she'd covered him with. "There is no way, under any circumstances, I sell to anyone—but most especially Gallagher. End of story."

She straightened her shoulders, fixing him with a determined gaze, the green of her hazel eyes seeming to blaze a little brighter.

"Everyone has a breaking point," she said, but it was no simple statement. That was a threat.

"I don't." He'd seen too many people's breaking points, and what broke *after* the fact. It wouldn't be him.

When a throat cleared, and it was neither his nor Dinah's, Carter was finally jerked out of whatever odd spell she had him under.

Jordan, his friend and the charter school science teacher who had a small group of children in uniforms behind him, was grinning at him from the other side of the gate. "Sorry to interrupt. But we have a field trip scheduled."

"Yes, Ms. Gallagher was just leaving."

Dinah lifted her chin slightly and gave the group a charming smile. "A field trip? You know, if you're looking for more opportunities in this area, Gallagher's Tap Room would always love to offer you a tour." She pulled a card from her sleek purse and handed it to Jordan.

Jordan, bless him, didn't take it. "As much as that would be very educational for our students, I'm not sure a tap room is the appropriate place for a middle school class. But thanks for the offer."

Dinah didn't wilt or frown or do anything to show that she'd just been denied. Her smile was frozen on her face, and Carter figured that was the extent of her reaction to rejection. To freeze. To pretend as though nothing had reached her.

He really hated that she could do that.

"Well, I'll leave you to your field trip then. It was a pleasure to meet you, and I'll see you again soon, Mr. Trask."

"No, you won't." But she was walking away with a little wave, as though she hadn't heard him. Well, he supposed that she *had* heard him, but she wasn't going to listen.

"Don't tell me Gallagher's is trying to ruin more of the city."

Carter grimaced at Jordan as the kids filed into the yard. He didn't *quite* agree with Jordan's assumption that Gallagher's was *ruining* anything. It couldn't be bad for the neighborhood to have some history, some restaurants that did well and brought in money.

But then again, Gallagher's was also the group trying to pave over his heart. What the hell was he doing trying to defend the devil?

"She's hot though."

Carter shook his head. "Don't we have kids to teach?" He nodded at the group of chattering school kids.

Jordan laughed, but he dropped the subject, leading the kids back to the shed where Carter would go through his presentation about the tools used to plant and harvest his crops. But he couldn't resist one last glimpse back to where Gallagher's loomed like the intimidating beast that it was.

*Everyone has a breaking point.*

She was probably right, but he'd be damned if she'd ever find his.

# Chapter 5

"Dinah, come on. You've got to let this go." Dinah looked up from her phone as Kayla slid into the booth across from her.

Five days of near constant obsessing about Carter Trask and she was no closer to new ideas for how to obtain his land, no new plans, and just a few too many fantasies about showing up at his doorstep again—very much as D. No Dinah Gallagher to be found.

"If you hadn't been late, I wouldn't have been sitting here with only my phone for company." Dinah forced herself to smile. "Girls' night begins now." Of course, as she slid her phone off the table and into her purse, she *might* have left the screen faceup on the off chance Kayla was distracted by something and she could finish her ten millionth Internet search on Carter Trask.

"Look, I know this is really important to you . . ." Kayla looked pained and let out a gusty breath. "But maybe it's time we accept the reality of the situation."

"What reality?" Dinah returned, frowning at her cousin.

"My dad is not giving up power like Grandmother gave it up for our dads. Craig Gallagher is going to hold on to DOO with everything he has, and he's doing everything he can to make sure you don't get it, ever. He's making sure I can't get anything done in my role. Maybe we accept that Gallagher's isn't going to be for us."

"What are you talking about?" Dinah demanded, phone and Trask forgotten for a few seconds. "This has been our dream forever. It's *tradition*. And the position you convinced them to create for you is great. We need sustainability, we need—"

Kayla looked down at her silverware, a miserable frown on her face. "Sustainability manager for a restaurant where management won't listen to a damn thing I have to say. Quite honestly, you're not listening to what I have to say either. I don't think building over Trask is right." Kayla glanced up, meeting Dinah's confused gaze with a certain bleakness and determination Dinah had never seen on Kayla's face.

"I don't think it's *right*," Kayla repeated, lightly tapping her fist against the table. "I think we should fail at this and accept we are not part of Gallagher's. There could be something else for us out there. Something real."

"Kayla, where is this coming from? This has been our life for . . . forever."

"Exactly. I am tired of the way our life is *Gallagher's*. Maybe our life should be something else. Something that some jackass Gallagher *man* can't sweep in and ruin."

"What happened?" Dinah demanded.

Kayla looked as if she was about to burst into tears, and as much as Dinah knew that her cousin was more emotional than she was, Kayla didn't get bent out of shape about silly things. Something was really, really going on. Dread settled in the pit of Dinah's stomach.

"Dad's trying to eliminate my position," she said on little more than a whisper.

"What? He can't—"

"They had a secret board meeting last night—one I only found out about because Barb thought I should have a heads-up. She told me Dad had a big presentation about how you're losing Trask, and without that, there's no farmers' market idea, and without *that*, there's no point in keeping me."

Thank goodness for Barb, the only woman on the board. "Why would he do that?"

"That's what I'm trying to tell you, Dinah. He doesn't want us." Kayla leaned across the table, tears glittering in her big blue eyes. "He doesn't want a younger generation. He wants to hold on to Gallagher's until he is dead, and then who knows." Kayla shook her head, and Dinah knew that look well. Kayla tried so hard not to be hurt by her cold father, but always failed.

Dinah reached across the table and grabbed Kayla's hand, giving it a reassuring squeeze. "We can't let him win this. We have to fight."

"You know I hate fighting. I always lose."

"No, that isn't true, and I'm not letting you go down without a fight. If I get Trask to sell, Craig can't get rid of you. So that's what I'll do, one way or another. You will keep your job, and I will become director, and then we can force *him* out. He's not doing what's best for Gallagher's. He's doing what's best for Craig."

"I don't want to fight my own father, and I don't feel right about fighting Carter Trask either. He seems like a nice guy with a cool idea. I read this article about this group he has, some sort of inner-city program where kids come and work on the farm in the summer to keep out of trouble. He seems like a genuinely good guy, and I don't want to be the one—"

"You have a big heart, Kay. I understand. But he can do the same thing somewhere else. We can't build this farmers' market somewhere else and still help our business. A business that will revitalize this neighborhood. We're doing good too, and . . . sometimes the world is good versus good, and one good guy has to lose. We have been here for over a century, Kayla. We belong here. It's our name and our life and we cannot let one Gallagher egomaniac beat us. I need you with me on this. I need you fighting by my side."

Kayla looked away, and Dinah knew she hadn't reached her. Kayla was lost in a world of personal hurt and emotional pain. Dinah didn't know how to reach her or how to help her, but she wasn't going to let Uncle Craig get rid of both of them. She wouldn't stand for it.

"I just want to go home. I'm sorry. I'm . . . I'm in no mood for girls' night. I'm in no mood for . . . I just want to go home. Sleep on it. Maybe I'll have a clearer head in the morning."

"Do you want me to come with? Make brownies? We can watch some terrible movie that we can make fun of. Ooh, *Step Up*."

Kayla gave the ghost of a smile. "I want to be alone. I'm sorry."

"You don't have to apologize to me for that." Dinah squeezed her hand again. "If you really want to be alone, I will give you that. Tonight."

"Just tonight?"

"Yes. Because I'm your cousin, and I love you, and you're my best friend. I won't let you wallow alone for more than one night. If you need two-night wallowing, the second night you get a visitor who will come bearing junk food and dance movies."

Kayla swallowed, and her smile was wobbly. "Thank you for being the best. But make sure you add wine to your list for tomorrow."

Dinah smiled in return, though hers didn't feel any more jovial. "You got it, sister."

Kayla slid out of the booth and came around to Dinah's side and gave her a quick hug. Dinah watched Kayla leave their little corner booth at Gallagher's, her attempt at a smile morphing into a scowl as fury pumped through her.

How dare that man do this? How dare both the men in their family just . . . She believed in Gallagher's like a religion. It was a living, breathing entity of history and a tool that could revitalize this crumbling neighborhood. And the Gallagher men were just using it for their own devices. Their own egos and whatever else made middle-aged men go absolutely insane.

Dinah couldn't let them win. She wouldn't let Kayla lose simply because Dinah hadn't gotten through to Carter yet. She had to find a way.

She slid her purse onto her shoulder and headed to the back. She'd go home and work all night if she had to, studying Carter Trask's life until *something* gave. She'd been going too easy on herself the past few days, indulging in too many fantasies.

That was over. Time to kick her own butt. She walked through the bustling back hallway next to the kitchen and exited through the back entrance. The employee parking lot was packed for the Friday night crowd, and Dinah didn't think anything of the man standing next to her car. A lot of times employees smoked out here even though they weren't supposed to, and she assumed it was just any other waiter on his break.

Until she got close enough for the lights of the parking lot to highlight the dark beard around his mouth. It was crazy that her heart did a little jitter and her stomach a little flip. Not dread or fear or anything other than excitement.

"You know we have cameras if you're planning on kidnapping me, then getting rid of me," she offered as dryly as her all-too-excited nerves would allow.

"That should have been the plan, come to think of it," Carter said in that dark, gravelly voice of his that surpassed any fictional voice she'd ever made up for him. "But thanks for the warning about cameras. I'll keep it in mind should my intentions turn nefarious."

She shouldn't want to smile. It wasn't funny, but more importantly, he was the enemy. She couldn't think about him as C anymore. He had to be Carter Trask, the man she had to break.

But there was a certain bleakness to his expression tonight that reminded her a little too much of what she'd seen in Kayla's eyes. Dinah had to swallow against the need to ask if everything was all right. Even if it wasn't, even if he was having his own personal crisis, that had nothing to do with her.

"I have written you about ten emails." He said it in a whoosh, as though he hadn't meant to confess that.

Dinah went to pull her phone out of her purse, but he shook his head. "I deleted them all before I sent them."

"Oh."

"The other night . . ."

"We agreed the other night didn't exist." She had to force her legs forward so she could grab her driver-side handle, but Carter stepped in the way, blocking her from her car.

Yes, she had slept with this man, and she had written one million messages to him. But the bottom line was she didn't know him, and there should be some sense of fear about the way he was blocking her from her vehicle. Except he wasn't touching her in any way. He wasn't threatening her. He was just standing in front of her. Looking a little too intensely lost.

"The other night when you came to my place, you were having a crisis, right?" he persisted.

"I guess you could call it a crisis." Which she shouldn't have said. She should have told him no and gotten in her car, but she stood there, desperately forcing herself not to reach out and touch him.

"My grandmother died," he said in another rush. "I knew it was coming. She's been in the nursing home for a while. I've spent three days trying to wrap my brain around her not being here anymore. And I can't. I can't get out of my head. I am in crisis, and all I wanted to do was email you. Which is sick and pathetic, I get that. Trust me."

Her chest hurt. It ached. She was surprised she had tears for a man she barely knew and for his grandmother whom she'd never met. She should turn around and disappear back into the restaurant. She should tell him that it didn't matter what crisis he was going through, they couldn't come back to C and D.

But she could remember the words he'd written about his grandmother's garden, how she'd taught him to make a special sauce he'd never made for anyone, but wanted to make for her.

They were there, unbidden, in her head, in her heart, and she wanted to give him what he'd given her last week. She shouldn't, but she *did*. So she reached out and touched her fingertips to his chest. "When you lose someone you love, I think sad and pathetic is what you get to be."

His desolate gaze met hers, and she could feel a shudder move through him. So she slid her hand up to his shoulder, rubbing up and down in what she hoped was some sort of comforting gesture.

She promised herself she wouldn't do this again, but weren't these extenuating circumstances? She would just be a comfort to him while he grieved for his grandmother. That didn't mean she wasn't still planning on getting his land, or that she'd given up on convincing him he was wrong. It just meant that, for a few hours, one more time, she got to be D instead of Dinah.

She could be the kind of woman a man would go to when he needed comfort. The kind of woman a man could lean on. For just once in her life, she could be the soft woman inside of her that she was always afraid to let lead.

It wasn't so wrong. It wasn't so bad. It was just a few hours of make-believe and pretend. That was all.

"I can follow you home."

"As D?"

It was her last chance to come to her senses. Her last chance to re-member everything she'd just decided inside of that restaurant.

But something about this man eradicated all that sense and all that determination. It crumbled the foundation of her drive and reminded her she was someone outside of Gallagher's, outside of her goals. All of those things were so exhausting, so tiring.

It was just too much to resist that for a few hours she wouldn't have to worry or think too hard. She wouldn't have to be perfect or have all the answers or save anyone.

She could just be her, and he could just be him. That fantasy be-tween them could give them what they both needed.

"D. Just D," she returned, her voice soft, everything inside of her soft and wanting, so the opposite of *Dinah*.

He gave a little nod of acknowledgment, and then they were walk-ing from the parking lot of Gallagher's, toward his little farm oasis in the middle of the city.

She knew they weren't dating. They weren't in a relationship, and they probably didn't even really know each other, but she couldn't resist sliding her hand into his and giving him a reassuring squeeze as they walked.

Carter was losing it. The last thing he should've done tonight was walk over to Gallagher's. But it had been there, *looming* in the distance, staring at him—the blinking beacon of what he wanted.

D. Fantasy. A life that didn't hurt so damn bad like this one did.

It was fucked up beyond belief that D was Dinah, and worse that they were pretending that they could set aside half their lives—no, more than half their lives—95 percent of their lives, and have this little 5 percent of messed-up sex.

But he didn't care. His heart hurt and he just had to get out of this space before all of that pain came crashing down inside of him.

His family had left this morning after the funeral yesterday, and that was part of the pain. That they could come and grieve, and then just leave. The way everyone always did. Everyone always taking everything and *leaving*.

But D's hand was in his, warm and alive. Other than his farm, her words had been the only constant, living thing in his life in the past few months. Everything had centered on starting the farm, then growing it the past few years, and she'd been the only one to penetrate that focus.

The fact she was real . . .

Maybe some other day he could focus on the messed-up part of all this, how she was irrevocably Gallagher and the enemy, but today he didn't have it in him. If he didn't let some of this pressure go, he would explode.

They reached his gate, having said absolutely nothing in the quick walk. He thought about offering her one last chance to back out. He thought about trying to affect some nonsense persona, someone who didn't give a shit if she wanted to stay or not. He almost told her to just go, that this was all a mistake.

But he didn't see the woman who had tried to buy his land out from under him next to him tonight. This woman had her hair back in a ponytail, and her makeup must have smudged off over the course of the day. She had a silky shirt on, jeans, and yeah, those ridiculous fashion boots women were always wearing these days, but she didn't look like Dinah Gallagher, ruler of her own little world.

She looked like any other woman. Soft and warm and approachable. So he didn't say a word, he just opened his gate, and she walked in ahead of him.

He was hard just from watching her saunter through his rows of plants that led to the door. The soft curve of her ass in those jeans, the way it felt like she'd walked that row, sauntered toward his porch, a million times before.

After all, how many times had he written this scenario? Coming home together, walking toward that house with sex on their minds. He'd imagined it in great detail over and over for months.

She didn't disappoint. Not in the least. He followed her at a leisurely pace, the pressure in his chest already unwinding. Sick. Pathetic. Sure. But if that's what fantasy could do, if it could get him through this boiling, painful grief, then he would use it. He would use C and D, even if it was wrong.

Hell, she'd started it. With her *What if I said I wanted you to fuck me?* that night, in his living room.

It was his turn to have his way. She took the stairs of his stoop with that confident grace that never seemed to leave her. She was standing at his door, giving him one of those little arched-brow looks he imagined worked on a million men in a million boardrooms. She was a force. Powerful. He wanted some of that for himself, even knowing it was from the last woman he could possibly want anything from and survive.

He took the stairs slowly, one by one, feeling something like a predator. And he liked it. He liked it because he could tell that she liked it. The way she inhaled sharply and gave a little sigh, the way she leaned slightly against his door, her breasts arching out as if they wanted to touch him.

He didn't stop. He kept going until he was pressed up against her pressed up against that door. Her palms were flattened against the rough wood and he pressed his on either side of her head.

Her breath came in short puffs and her eyes all but glowed green in the porch light. She smelled like a mix of citrusy perfume and the greasy bar food of Gallagher's. It was a strangely erotic combination because it was strangely revealing. Polished, pretty Dinah Gallagher in her pencil skirts and high heels and probably expensive perfume, managing what really wasn't much more than a glorified bar.

Except that didn't matter. Not the Dinah Gallagher part of her. He didn't want that. He wanted D, this fantasy person.

He didn't move. He let the moment stretch out, drawing tighter and tighter as their gazes held. He ached for her, and there was something deliciously potent in that. Potent enough to make him forget what this was all about. Who she was. Who he was. All he could feel was the steady throb of his dick. All he could see was the lust in her gaze, and all he could feel was the sweet softness of D.

He wanted to live in this moment. Soak it up. Stay here—right here in heady anticipation. But she moved, her hands coming off the door, reaching out, her fingers slowly curling under the waistband of his jeans. He could feel the slight scrape of her nails against the sensitive skin at his hips.

The little sound of satisfaction she made flashed through him like a sweet burn. Her fingers edged toward the center and she deftly flicked the button open and then undid the zipper. Her finger traced the rock-hard outline of him. Again she made that little pleasured noise and this time he groaned too.

She laughed, something sweet and bright about it that lifted him up out of the darkness he'd been struggling so hard to rise above.

He shouldn't do this. He didn't deserve this, and yet he couldn't walk away.

"Do you remember the one where we started out here?"

As though one of their little scenarios was a memory instead of a few typed words. But something about their exchanges had always been like memory.

"I think I recall," he said dryly. Because of course he remembered. He remembered all of it. Too much, too clearly, especially now that he had this vision of the real D to impose over all those old images. Now he could see it all, with her, as if it actually happened.

Her finger trailed down the length of him and back up again, her eyes mischievous and bright. "Do you think your neighbor would mind?"

"I'll keep my eyes open for any window peepers."

"I think it's only considered window peeping if you're outside looking in."

He took one hand off the door, the strength of his other hand the only thing keeping him upright in the face of Dinah's practically offering to blow him on his front porch.

He was a man. He wasn't going to refuse the insinuated offer. He pushed some of the stray strands of hair off her forehead and then raked his fingers through the top of her ponytail. Then he gave her a gentle nudge on the top of her head.

Her smile spread, wide and gorgeous, and he wasn't sure how long he would last with that sweet mouth on his cock, but he needed it like oxygen.

Slowly, acting the tease she'd always claimed to be in her emails, she lowered herself farther and farther down until she was on her knees, on his porch, for him.

They were angled so the porch light was behind him, keeping her in shadow. Not that he could muster up the brainpower to care if someone might walk by and see what was happening.

She tugged his jeans down to midthigh and then pulled the waistband of his boxers away from his abdomen so that she could pull the thick length of him out. She curled her hand around him. Hot. Soft. Perfect. She looked up at him through dark lashes, the curve of a dangerous smile still lighting up her face. She stuck out her tongue and rubbed the tip across her top lip before starting at the very base of him. Lightly, all too lightly, she licked up to the head.

His fingers tightened in her hair, and she groaned in approval, so he didn't loosen his hold. He held her there, urging her face closer.

"Open that hot little mouth for me."

She groaned again, all pleasure, all approval. It was insane this excitement between them. They could say things like that and not feel one jolt of embarrassment.

Or maybe it was just that she did exactly as he said and opened her mouth. For *him*. Sucking him deep into all that wet, delicious heat. So deep he had to close his eyes just to keep upright, just to think, just to breathe.

But he forced himself to open them after that, to watch her take him in, slow and deep, and then out again. Her gaze held his the entire time, as though she got something out of what he could only assume was an expression of pure, unadulterated pleasure on his face.

Her tongue teased as she drove him further and further away from sanity. Which was exactly where he wanted to be. As far away from sanity and reality as he could get.

He could feel the orgasm coiling around him, and he could try to fight it off, he could try to get her there first, but that wasn't what they'd emailed that time.

She'd wanted him to be so excited he couldn't hold back. She'd written some truly filthy stuff about getting him off. Remembering that had him moving his hips with her.

"I'm going to come, D." A warning. A chance for her to back off or away. To go inside instead of bringing him to orgasm in the chilly night air.

Her gaze met his and she didn't stop. If anything she moved faster, harder. He couldn't hold it off—the pleasure that overcame him, through him. The bursting, bright release and her taking it all, easily, maybe even enthusiastically.

His ears were ringing by the time he slowly eased out of her mouth, and he wasn't sure he would consider himself steady on his feet.

There was a new need inside of him now. A need to give. To drive her just as crazy as she drove him. He jerked her to her feet and grabbed his keys out of his pocket.

"The second we're inside, your clothes better be off because I'm going to make you come all over my mouth."

She grinned at him, doing the tongue thing again where the tip of her tongue traced her upper lip. He jammed the key in the lock and shoved the door open, nudging her inside.

As she stepped forward, she was already taking off her shirt. She was wearing a very serviceable white bra, nothing like all of the lacy, frilly lingerie she'd described to him over the past few months. But even simple underwear did nothing to lessen the punch that was D.

She pulled off her boots, then shimmied out of her jeans, taking her underwear with it. Without hesitation, she unclasped her bra and dropped it so she was standing naked in front of him.

Freckles and acres of pale skin, the rosy tips of her nipples gathered in a tight bud he wanted to bite. But first . . . first, he was going to make her scream.

He advanced on her and she just stood there and smiled at him as he grabbed her. He devoured her mouth as though he were a drowning man. Because that's what it felt like. Only this kind of drowning was perfect. Everything he needed.

He managed to wrench his mouth away from hers and gestured

toward the rug. "Get on the floor." He didn't soften the rough note in his voice, and she obeyed.

He pulled off his shirt as she lay down. He kneeled at her feet, curling his fingers around her ankles and slowly spreading them apart before sliding his hands up her calves and thighs, his body following until his mouth was only inches from where he planned to devour her now.

He could smell her arousal, sweet and earthy, and it was everything to have her here at his mercy, where he could taste her and drive her into screaming, writhing orgasm.

And that's just what he set out to do.

# Chapter 6

Dinah had never had sex that wasn't in a bed. It was an odd thought to have, lying on Carter's floor, his hands sliding up her legs, his mouth devilishly close to where she wanted him most.

Mouth, fingers, cock. She wanted all of him, all over her. She wanted all of him until she was nothing but a writhing mass of ecstasy. The thing was, she believed he could do that.

On the floor. On the porch. She believed in his talents, and as his tongue licked up the center of her she couldn't have spelled her last name if her life depended on it. More, she didn't want to remember much of anything that had to do with Gallagher or Trask.

He used his finger and tongue interchangeably in some kind of pattern she couldn't find a rhythm to. It was that inability to find a rhythm that made it somehow more exciting and mind scrambling. She didn't care that she was naked on his living room floor; all she cared about were the sensations shooting through her. She could feel the rough scrape of his whiskers against her inner thighs as he licked and sucked her toward some kind of oblivion. She scraped her fingernails through his hair and across his scalp and was rewarded by an exhale of breath against her.

She pressed herself against his mouth in a way that should be embarrassing, but she couldn't manage it when she was so close to tumbling over that peak. She'd already been close just from having her mouth on him, from feeling his pleasure when she took him deep inside of her mouth. She'd felt powerful and sexy and like she had given him something and taken something for herself at the same time.

It was remembering kneeling on his rough porch with his cock in her mouth, and the final flick of his all too devastating tongue, that sent her over a keening, wild edge. One that she wildly and enthusiastically groaned her way through.

He hooked his arms around her thighs, holding her almost impossibly still as he drove her over the last peak, teasing out those last waves of pleasure.

She was breathing heavily and staring at the ceiling and not quite sure how to ever come down from the immeasurable high her body was currently feeling. He leaned over her, holding himself above her with those suitably impressive arms.

She blinked up at him, completely and utterly relaxed and satisfied. She trailed her palm across his beard. There was something about the rough scrape against her skin that was oddly . . . comforting?

No, that couldn't be the right word. She was just sex muddled.

"Come on now." With an ease that shouldn't have delighted her, but did anyway, he hefted her up off the floor and over his shoulder. But he didn't take her into the bedroom as she'd expected; instead he stepped into his little kitchen.

He plopped her on the counter as though she weighed less than nothing. "Did you eat any dinner?" he demanded in that gruff voice that sent a little shiver down her spine.

"Dinner? Well, no."

He shook his head and stalked over to the refrigerator. "You're going to eat."

"Is that a metaphor?"

He shook his head, though he smiled as he looked over his shoulder at her. "No. You're going to eat some food. Then . . ." That smile widened into a full-blown grin, and her stomach flipped, a delicious swoop of . . .

It was like sex, and not like it at all. Something warm and comforting in that pleasure. Something bigger.

So not what she needed, or anything she should enjoy or nurture. She needed to get out of there. She needed to forget that this weird alternate reality actually existed. She needed to get off his counter, put on her clothes, and leave.

But he was pulling food out of his refrigerator, shirtless and barefoot and gorgeous. How did someone walk away from *that*?

When he was done puttering, he handed her a bowl and a fork.

She wrinkled her nose at all that *green*. "Is that kale?" She squinted her eyes at him. "Are you trying to kill me?"

"Very funny. Eat it."

"It's just that I'm deathly allergic to green veg—ooh, is that bacon?"

"Eat, princess."

She grinned, but complied. She might prefer a hamburger over a random conglomeration of greens and some kind of bacon dressing, but it wasn't half bad, and more, she knew he'd grown almost everything in her bowl, and there was something kind of special about that.

*About him.*

She blinked at the salad, focusing on it instead of him, because she couldn't have thoughts like that.

He'd gotten himself an almost identical bowl of whatever this magical mix was that made greens not taste quite so green.

The silence that settled over them wasn't completely unwelcome, but the fact that she was on his counter, eating, *naked*, felt a little weird. Not necessarily because she wasn't clothed, which was a surprise, but more because silence gave her time to think. About how he had come to her. About how he'd needed something from her.

Thinking about that made her sad for him all over again. How he'd lost his grandmother and didn't know how to come to grips with his grief.

But unfortunately she didn't feel quite right about saying *Sorry about your dead grandma* when she was sitting here naked on the counter. Yeah, that wasn't going to work.

"I don't suppose you have any cake? Pie? I'd even settle for a muffin with chocolate in it."

"If it doesn't grow from my garden, I don't have it."

"How is that even possible? You need like . . . salt and flour and *coffee*! And—"

"I don't drink coffee."

"You don't . . . You don't drink coffee."

"No. Never have."

"I'm trying to understand how that's physically possible. Are you an alien? That would make much more sense than a human who doesn't drink coffee."

His mouth curved and she got no simple pleasure from the fact she could make him smile. Especially now. It was one of those things she wasn't allowed to feel about him. Because he was the enemy. The man whose land she was supposed to buy.

It was funny how they could justify it to themselves to have these two separate identities. C and D, Carter and Dinah. Was it so crazy to think that justification could continue . . . a little bit longer? Yes, she was still trying to buy his land, but she hadn't been sexed out of that idea yet. Maybe this was simply something they could do. She studied him until he glared at her.

"What?"

"Nothing. Just trying to work out why you've been feeding me."

"You figure it out?"

"You're secretly the nicest guy on the face of the planet?"

"Try again."

"The kale actually *is* poison and you're going to kill me so I can't buy your land?" It was something of a test to see if he would wince or cringe or lose that easy looseness about him that only seemed to come out after they'd had sex.

"Not yet." He stepped toward her, setting his bowl and then hers on the counter. He spread her legs wide with those big, rough hands, and then stepped between her legs. The height of the counter didn't leave for easy matching of their bodies, but he could rub the rough edge of his denim against the wet heat of her pussy.

She spread her legs wider, ready and willing for whatever he was offering. It should concern her how much she wanted him, how *easy* she was when he was this way, and yet even in the light of day she had trouble finding that shame. "So, why'd you feed me then?"

"I wanted to make sure you wouldn't wimp out on me. Get some energy before round two."

"Do you think I can't handle round two?" she asked with an arched brow.

He flashed her that sexy-as-sin grin that was in no way fair. "Oh, I have all the faith in the world in you there, D." He lifted her and she wrapped her legs around his waist as he walked her to the bedroom.

Carter was not a stupid man, though he'd been told on occasion that he was. There were times people mistook his drive and his determination for an inability to see reason. He had never believed it.

Until now.

Carrying Dinah to his bedroom, and before that feeding her, talking to her, treating her like a woman he cared about, was idiotic and stupid and against everything he knew he had to do.

But he didn't stop. He carried her to his bed, and he laid her on the mattress with a care he shouldn't afford her. He planned on fucking her for as long as he possibly could. No amount of argument from his brain seemed to stop this fire she unleashed in him. It was a feeling that had been so elusive in his life. Something like belonging.

He knew it was as fleeting as those things he'd belonged to in his life—the farms, the people. There was no way in any universe this worked out. No way this went beyond a couple of stupid mistakes in the bedroom.

But he couldn't stop.

He covered her body with his, absorbing the soft way her body gave in to his. Exulting in this feeling of connection that she gave him.

Tonight, for this little period of time, he was just going to consider her his. His fantasy. His dream come to life. The rest of it didn't matter, and he wasn't going to let it matter. He was going to get through this suffocating grief by finding pleasure somewhere. In D.

Without getting off of her, he reached over and found the box of condoms he'd purchased earlier knowing this was the only way . . . When even farming wouldn't take the edge off of his grief, he knew that this was all he had. A million deleted emails, and the fact was, he needed the reality now. The reality of her.

He shoved apart his still unbuttoned and unzipped jeans and tugged down his boxers. But before he could sheath himself, Dinah plucked the condom wrapper out of his hands and ripped the packet open, pulling the condom out. With her bottom lip between her teeth, slowly and agonizingly, she rolled the condom onto his erection.

She was the sexiest woman he'd ever known, adventurous and mischievous, sweet and dirty, this perfect mix of a million things, and it was too much, really. She was, in her entirety, too damn much. Enough *too much* to pause, to question . . .

"What was your favorite one?" she asked, her fingers delicately trailing up and down his arms.

"My favorite one?" He knew what she meant. His favorite fantasy. His favorite of whatever scenarios they'd written to each other. But it was hard to choose for a lot of reasons. Each exchange between them had been a reaction to something going on in his life. A certain need, and it was a little embarrassing to admit that today he didn't need anything dark or dirty particularly. He just needed someone, and in this case, that someone had to be her. Had to be.

She reached out and pushed some hair off his forehead, a comforting and familiar gesture. A gesture of care they didn't share. Couldn't. Something that spoke of a deeper relationship than they had. All they had were fake words.

"I always have a hard time picking a favorite," she said when he never answered. "It sort of depends on the situation, doesn't it?"

It wasn't a shock she would echo his own thoughts. For whatever ways their whole thing was a fantasy built on randomly exchanged emails, there had been a truthfulness to some of their words. A truthfulness he hadn't even admitted to himself at the time, but it was easy to confide in this person who wasn't real. This person he'd never know.

Except here she was. She was here and real and this was far more complicated than the fantasy had ever been.

But he wasn't walking away from that complication. No, he kept going headlong into it, no matter how often, during the daylight hours, he told himself to stay away.

He didn't want to think up one of his favorites, and he didn't want to think about complications and hardships. All he wanted to do was lose himself in her. So instead of answering her question or responding to her statement, he dropped his mouth to hers.

He didn't say anything. Not as he kissed her, softly, languorously, exploring her mouth with no hurry or frenzy. He didn't speak as his mouth drifted down her neck to the soft swell of her breasts. Not as he entered her and breathed in her sweet little sigh.

There were no words and no fake memories. There was only the soft slide of his body against hers. Only the tender brush of her palms and fingertips up and down his back. They didn't race. They didn't play. It was something deeper, and more, and no matter how much he knew he couldn't afford those things, it was exactly what he needed in this moment.

When she came, it was soft and sweet and sighing. And when he came, it was the same.

He kicked off his pants and moved next to her on the bed, more than a little bit reluctant to roll away from her and go to clean himself up.

But it wasn't like the other night when she'd scurried off his bed and he'd gotten off of her immediately. Instead, they both lay there. Their shoulders touching, their legs brushing, but not exactly cuddling or curling into each other.

Carter stared at the ceiling, and when he dared to sneak a glance at her, she was doing the same.

But she didn't get up to move, and even though he shouldn't— couldn't—he pressed a kiss to her temple and whispered the last word he should ever utter in this situation.

"Stay."

When he rolled off the bed to get rid of the condom, he wasn't all that sure she would listen. He wasn't sure he *wanted* her to listen. He only knew that . . . that . . . Scratch that. He knew nothing. He knew nothing at all.

When he came back from the little bathroom, she was still lying naked on his bed. Still staring at the ceiling, clearly not quite certain this was what she should be doing.

But still here, doing it anyway.

He slid next to her on the bed, and this time he wrapped an arm around her. She curled into him. It was a mistake on every level, but neither of them made a move to fix it.

# Chapter 7

Dinah woke up in a bed that was not her own and cursed herself silly. Of all the epic mistakes in her life, this really topped the list. Sleeping with him . . . It had been excusable the first time. She might've even been able to rationalize it the second time.

There was nothing excusable or able to be rationalized about spending the night in Carter Trask's bed. So many things could go wrong here, and why was she risking what she loved above all else? Just because the man knew how to give her a couple of orgasms?

On the plus side, Carter was not in bed next to her. She woke up in his bed completely alone.

How that was the plus side, she had no idea. Clearly she had no idea about anything if she was, you know, here. She was tempted to roll face-first into the pillow and scream until something in her life made sense. Instead, she got out of bed and looked around and realized none of her clothes were in the room.

Damn it. She would have to find something of Carter's to put on so she could get her clothes from the living room. Carter's living room. In the morning. Morning with a man who didn't drink coffee and wouldn't sell her his land, which she needed in order to save not just her dream, but her cousin's as well.

She'd certainly picked a hell of a time to have whatever quarter-life crisis this was.

The bedroom door squeaked open and Carter stuck his head in.

"Good. You're up." He stepped forward, a bundle of clothes in his arms. "I've got your clothes."

His eyes drifted to her naked breasts and she was stupid enough to get a little tingly over that. Stupid enough to remember and wonder if she had time to indulge herself in—no.

"What time is it?" she asked, reaching out for her clothes.

He didn't hand them over. "Five thirty," he returned, definitely *not* making eye contact.

"In the morning?"

He smiled even as he rolled his eyes. There was something kind of sweet about the smile, the eye roll.

She didn't want to dwell on that.

"My workday begins at four thirty. I figured you'd want to get back to your place and shower before you have to go to work, but maybe not quite that early."

He finally offered the clothes, though not without one last glance up and down. She took the outstretched garments, looking at him helplessly. She felt helpless and kind of silly, actually. Two things she hadn't allowed herself to feel possibly ever.

But recently life kept shoving these experiences at her as if it was determined she had to feel them.

"Thank you feels weird to say about sex, but I . . . wanted to thank you about the overall gesture last night," Carter offered somberly.

"You don't thank someone for a gesture," she returned. It hadn't been an obligation or even a *gesture* exactly. It had been . . .

"Even your work enemy?"

"You think there are rules about work enemies? I could probably use a few. I think I'm doing it terribly wrong." Which was very annoying when it felt so damn right.

Again he smiled, his gaze missing nothing as it swept over her still naked body. "Well, work enemy, if you want to remain enemies in the daylight hours, you're going to have to get dressed."

Why was he so tempting? She pressed the tip of her tongue to the corner of her mouth, feeling more than gratified when he groaned. "Not today. Not during the day. That's the rule. That needs to be a rule." She said it aloud, but it was far more to herself than to him.

"Does that mean that at night . . ."

No. She couldn't allow it. She had to make this the end of whatever weird personal thing they were to each other. There was too much at stake. "Carter . . ."

It was the fact he was struggling with it too that perhaps broke her brain a little bit. When she'd look back on this moment later, she'd definitely think her brain had broken. "Maybe . . . at night, we're C and D, and if they happen to run into each other, who are Dinah and Carter to . . . complicate matters?"

"You mean aside from the fact they're work enemies and not actually separate people from C and D?"

"Possibly."

He shook his head. "It's amazing what sex makes people do." But he had that *smile*, that lightness to him. A warmth she didn't know how to resist.

She had to laugh. It was so absurd and he was so . . . charming, somehow, in this weird, gruff way of his. He made her laugh and feel special and kind of weirdly warm and squirmy.

"You should get out of here."

Yes, staying a second longer was ludicrous. It was foolish. She had work to do and it was all she could possibly care about.

"If C and D made plans to see each other at night, would Carter and Dinah have an issue with that?" she blurted instead.

He blinked and his expression shuttered a little bit. Enough so that she wished she hadn't said it. She wished she could get her head on straight around him, but she was naked. She needed to fix that. She started pulling on her clothes and tried to ignore the fact that Carter still hadn't answered her.

"What are you doing tonight?"

She whipped her head up to stare at him, all deer-caught-in-headlights like. She knew she should say no. She should say she was busy and they couldn't do this and there had to be a boundary.

Not this whole day-and-night boundary nonsense, but like a real all-the-time boundary, because this was like playing with fire. Somehow . . . somehow everyone was going to get burned in the process, and she didn't want any part of that.

"D's got no plans," she said despite all the rational thoughts in her head. Because Carter was right, it was amazing what sex could make people do. "Maybe she could go for a walk outside of Gallagher's, say, around eight?"

Carter seemed to consider this very, very seriously. He was putting far too much thought into an answer. Or maybe it was exactly the right amount of thought. The thought she wasn't giving this situation, clearly. Maybe he would be sensible enough to stop this insanity.

"Maybe I'll take a walk around there myself."

"You mean C will."

Again there was that odd expression on his face, something un-readable. Something she was glad she couldn't read.

He shrugged. "Yeah, C."

"Well then I will say goodbye as D. Because these are two separate lives that we're leading. Dinah and Carter don't exist here."

Surprisingly, he smiled. "Look, it doesn't make any sense."

"No, it doesn't."

"I mean, how long does this reasonably last? Eventually it'll get confusing, or too complicated or something, but for now why not just keep enjoying it until it's impossible to enjoy? I'm not sure there are a lot of things in my life I've ever just sort of let go and enjoyed."

Enjoy? Let *go*? Haha. Yeah, no. "Me neither."

"Then why not be hopelessly stupid motherfuckers who will live to regret this very decision?"

She laughed outright, and he smiled and laughed too and . . . damn it. Why not? Well, actually she wouldn't ask herself that question because she knew the many, many why-nots. "All right, C. I think, in this arena, we have a deal. Would you like to seal it with a handshake?"

He glanced at the watch on his wrist and then grinned at her. A full-on grin, and she knew what he was going say, and she knew she should avoid it and not at all be turned on by it.

"Shaking hands is *not* what I want to do on it."

"Responsible, business-minded Dinah Gallagher would flat-out refuse that horrible attempt at innuendo."

"And D?"

She glanced through the crack between the curtains and the window and noticed the world outside was still dusky. She grinned back at him.

"D rules the dark hours, and it appears it's still dark." She dropped her clothes, and in seconds they were tangled on the bed, kissing and laughing, and the Dinah voice of reason in her head was incredibly silent on the matter.

Carter made it through the day feeling surprisingly upbeat. There were some moments of grief definitely, things that snuck up on him— like the death of a basil plant, or thinking he smelled his grandmother's perfume.

But there was a lightness to him today that hadn't been there yesterday. He didn't feel quite so weighed down. Sad, yes, but not broken by it.

He knew exactly why that was, and he knew exactly why that made him a fucking idiot. And possibly certifiable.

"Hey, Carter."

Carter stood up from behind his bean plants to find Jordan standing at his fence. "Hey, Jordan. What's up, man?"

Jordan opened the gate and entered Carter's yard. He made his way to Carter through the rows of produce. It wasn't unusual for Jordan to stop by unannounced since his grandmother was Carter's neighbor; they'd become friends and had worked together on their summer urban-farming-for-kids program. But the next words out of his friend's mouth were not what Carter expected.

"I wanted to talk to you about the Gallaghers."

Carter tensed, and not for all the reasons he *should* have tensed. It should be all about *hating* the Gallaghers, and not about . . . Dinah. "What about them?"

"I've got some ideas on how we can fight them," Jordan said with a little too much fervor. Enough so that Carter laughed.

"We?"

"Yeah, man. I got your back. This is my neighborhood too. If they get you, they'll go after my grandma next," Jordan said, jerking his chin toward Carter's neighbor. "I'm not going to let them bulldoze you. For your sake, and hers, and mine. Not to even mention how important our summer program is. It's necessary, man. I'm in. I'm on your side, and I'm gonna help."

Carter could only stand there, somewhat stunned. Though he and Jordan had become friends over the course of Carter's building up the place here and Jordan's visiting his grandmother, Carter never would've expected someone to stand with him. Fight with him. He wouldn't have asked anyone to. He wouldn't have dreamed of it.

His whole adolescence he'd asked people to fight with him—to not sell, to not give in—but no one had. He'd been brushed off or, worse, ridiculed. He'd been told he was irrational or a dreamer or whatever else.

No one had ever, *ever* said *Yes, you're right, Carter. We have to fight. We have to make a stand.* No one had ever, *ever* had his damn back.

"Thanks, man," Carter forced himself to say, surprised at the depth of emotion he felt at Jordan's easy offer of help—no, not even offer. Jordan was standing there saying he had his back.

It was a big thing. Big enough he had to clear his throat to say more. "I appreciate the offer, I do, but I don't need help on this. My no isn't changing. I'm not selling to Gallagher. Ever."

"You don't know Gallagher if you think you don't need help," Jordan said, pacing the little brick pathway along the rows of beans. "They're the thing that has endured in this neighborhood, and you know why? Because they're shady as fuck. We're not going to let them take any more of this block."

"This place means too much to me, and it always has. There's nothing Gallagher can do. They can throw millions at me, they can be shady as whatever, but I'm not leaving. Money doesn't matter to me. Not anymore." He'd struggle through whatever for this land, no matter what. If he had to go into debt up to his eyeballs, if he had to beg his family to chip in, he'd do *anything* to keep this place.

"Okay, but keep your eyes open. Sometimes with people like that, you can't just say no. You've got to fight dirty."

"There's no fight, Jordan. No one's threatening me. No one's . . . I said no to them—to many of them—and that's that. They can't force my hand."

Jordan shrugged as he looked off in the direction of Gallagher's. "For now," he muttered, clearly unconvinced. "I'm starting to think it's better to go offensive than defensive with people like that. They're not just going to stop with this farmers' market. They're going to make this whole neighborhood hipster nonsense."

"I hate to break it to you, Jordan, but you're standing in a little bit of hipster nonsense as we speak."

Jordan chuckled. "Okay, fair, but you know what I mean. Cafés and apartments and yuppie bullshit they'll abandon at the first shooting. They don't want community, they want . . . Instagram shit." Jordan jerked a chin toward Gallagher's this time. "And they'll make money off it either way."

Carter looked over at the looming brick form of Gallagher's too. He knew Dinah wasn't sleeping with him to "play dirty," because it wasn't going to work. Whatever her reason was, it was separate.

Even so, Jordan's insinuation that they needed to fight the Gallaghers bothered him, more than it should. He shouldn't think about Dinah or what fighting dirty would mean to *her*, because he could only care about his own interests.

He only *did* care about his own interests. Any prick of guilt over Dinah was just some weird sex side-effect that would go away soon enough.

He wasn't caving. This thing with Dinah and/or D wasn't caving or giving in. It was separate. "Look, Jordan, I really appreciate your offer to help. If I get to the point where I feel like I have to fight to survive, I'll definitely give you a call. I can't lose this place, no matter what, but I don't think we have to stoop to fighting dirty."

Because he didn't want to fight. He just wanted to be. Raise his plants and sell his produce and live in this last place his family had roots.

It had absolutely zero to do with any pretty Gallaghers with ridiculously dirty fantasies.

Jordan shrugged again, still glaring toward Gallagher's. "I get it. Long as you know that I'm here and want to fight for you. This neighborhood's got to stand for something again. You're part of that."

"I take it seriously," Carter said gravely, because suddenly he was feeling grave. Grave and a bunch of other things he couldn't untangle. He'd never been a part of something. He'd always been the lone voice of opposition, the only one fighting to save his world.

"Good." Jordan clapped him on the back. "Come out with us tonight, huh?"

Carter's gaze drifted to Gallagher's. He couldn't help himself. He definitely should take the offer of friendship that was being handed to him instead of thinking that he had agreed to be walking around Gallagher's parking lot later. To meet D.

*Dinah Gallagher.*

But no amount of sense or reason was going to prevail today. It didn't stand a chance after last night. "I've got plans tonight, but Saturday? At Stars?"

"You got it. I'll see you later. Hey, you got anything I can bring to my grandma so she doesn't smack me for skipping out on church last week?"

Carter smiled and pointed toward his late-season melons in the back. "Yeah. Come with me."

# Chapter 8

Dinah had felt strange all day. Distracted. Confused. Daydreamy. All things she almost never was. Though if Craig or Grandmother noticed, they didn't say anything, which in Dinah's estimation meant they didn't notice.

But *she* noticed, and it was irritating the hell out of her that she could be distracted at the worst possible moment.

She raked her fingers through her hair, sitting at Kayla's desk, scowling at Craig's list of bitch chores for her, and far too often drifting off into memories of this morning. It was so much better than calling some distributor to turn the screws, or running to the post office.

This morning Carter had made her *beg* for release. She was pretty sure she had a bite mark on her shoulder. She knew she'd left a few marks on him. She tried to fight away a smile. She was at *work*. She could not be smiling over sex. Especially not over sex with *that* partner.

"This is the last thing you can be thinking about, Dinah Gallagher," she muttered aloud, trying to kick her brain into full-focused gear.

"What is?"

Dinah jerked in her seat and made a little screech of surprise. "Kayla. You scared me."

"I gathered," Kayla said with a smile as she stepped into the office and closed the door behind her. "You don't usually mutter to yourself so much unless Dad's been by, and I know he's been off-site all afternoon. What on earth has you so worked up?"

*Oh, just fucking Carter Trask. No, not as an adjective. As a verb. No big deal. We're two separate personalities.* Dinah barely resisted the urge to groan again. "I'm . . ."

"Worried?" Kayla asked, her eyebrows drawing together, her fingers linking, everything about her expression and posture radiating concern—and something Dinah couldn't quite put her finger on.

"No." Which was a lie, and she did hate to lie to Kayla, but Kayla was . . . softer. She needed someone very certain and strong to hold her up. That had always been Dinah's role.

"You don't need to worry about my welfare, because I've decided to start looking for other jobs."

"Kayla!" Dinah pushed away from Kayla's desk, sputtering and advancing on her cousin.

But Kayla straightened her shoulders and didn't cower at all. "This place is making me miserable, and—"

"But *we're* Gallagher's!"

"No, Dinah. I'm . . . me. I'm tired of all this business. I'm tired of Gallagher's and the restaurant and I'm tired of the way our family gives everything to this pile of brick and metal without ever giving anything to each other."

"Hey, that isn't fair. I—"

"I don't mean you, Dinah, but . . ."

"But what?"

Kayla rubbed her fingers over her forehead. "You're on your way. You're on your way to giving everything to this, and I don't like it for you, but most especially I don't like it for me. I tried to tell you last night and . . . I can't *do* this."

"Why are you giving him what he wants?" Dinah very nearly pounded a fist on Kayla's desk, except just in time the gesture reminded her of her father. And Craig.

She swallowed, cradling her clenched fist instead trying to figure out how Kayla could betray her like this. "How can you walk away?"

"Because I care more about my sanity than a name on a building, Dinah. I don't want to be them in twenty years. I don't want to be them *now*. I want . . . a life. One that doesn't require fighting my father every step of the way."

"That's what he wants!"

"I don't care," Kayla burst out in return, flinging her arms in the air. "You don't seem to get it, and you get to keep fighting, I'm not saying *you* shouldn't, but I'm not going to. I don't care who wants what, I'm tired of being miserable for a *building*."

"It's more than a building. It's our family. Our birthright. Our blood and roots are in this restaurant."

"For you," Kayla returned, firm and somehow hurt, or something very close. "I don't feel the same way anymore."

"You did."

She shook her head sadly and Dinah felt strangely like crying. Kayla had always been her partner, her co-dreamer. They'd had *plans.* How could she walk away from them?

"If I did feel that way, that feeling died, but I think mostly I just wanted to belong somewhere, and you were the only one willing. This was always the thing you wanted, so I convinced myself I wanted it too. But I never felt what you felt. Not really."

Dinah had to lean against the desk to keep herself upright. She couldn't believe this. She couldn't *understand* this. "Is something else going on? What aren't you telling me?"

Kayla rolled her eyes. "I'm telling you everything. I'm sorry if it's not what you want to hear, but it's a truth I've been ignoring for a long time. I'm tired of ignoring it. I'm most definitely tired of this." She swept her hand around the office as if she didn't see what Dinah saw.

History and belonging and *theirs.*

"I would appreciate it if you didn't tell my father I'm looking elsewhere until I've secured something else," Kayla continued, all polite businesswoman.

Dinah swallowed, hurt not just at Kayla's decision—wrong decision—but hurt she'd think Dinah would ever tell Craig anything they'd discussed. "I still love you, Kayla. I'd never hurt you."

Kayla smiled thinly. "Good. I hope . . . I hope it stays that way."

"Kay—"

But Kayla shook her head, looking close enough to tears to make Dinah feel perilously close herself.

"I'm going to go home. If Dad comes by, feel free to tell him I took off early. And you don't have to worry about coming over tonight. I won't be wallowing. I'm not wallowing anymore." With that, Kayla reopened her office door and left.

Dinah blinked, inwardly cursing herself for having forgotten she had plans with Kayla in the first place. Maybe Kayla was right and she'd gotten too deep in the Gallagher's nonsense . . .

Except how could that *be?* She was meeting with Carter tonight. Pretending she had two separate sides of her. Kayla's estimation was wrong, and if she didn't understand what Gallagher's meant, that wasn't Dinah's failing or Dinah being wrong.

She couldn't believe Kayla had been lying to her all these years, or just convincing herself she cared about Gallagher's; she was just scared. Craig was a bully, and he wasn't afraid to bully his own daughter.

Well, let Kayla look for a new job; Dinah was going to keep fighting. Even if she had to do it alone. She would prove to Kayla it was worth it, that Gallagher's *did* matter, and when Kayla came to her senses, Dinah would welcome her back without one *I told you so.*

Because no matter what was going on with Kayla or Carter or her father or Craig, Dinah would never, ever doubt Gallagher's was hers. She'd fight until the bitter end—and the only acceptable end was her running Gallagher's.

Carter cursed himself as he walked toward Gallagher's in the quickly darkening twilight. Jordan's visit had been a thorn in his side all day, one he couldn't get out of his skin.

Of course, that was exactly how Dinah—*D*—affected him too. Something about her had an unshakeable grasp on him.

No, Jordan's words were a thorn. Dinah Gallagher was a tick in the center of his back, a parasite who'd dug in and couldn't be ripped off without help.

He should be super charming and lead with that comparison.

Except as he reached Gallagher's imposing form and turned the corner to the back parking lot, Dinah was stepping out of the heavy door. Both the fading light and the orange glow of the parking lot lights bounced off the reds in her hair and made her look a little bit otherworldly.

*Witch* or *fairy* was far more fitting. Something so beautiful and spellbinding, his brain and reason had gone completely and utterly missing.

When she caught a glimpse of him and smiled, something inside of him shifted and lightened. She walked toward him, her legs looking impossibly edible in that tight knee-length skirt and killer heels.

Nothing in his entire life had ever snuck under the defenses he'd built to keep himself moving forward to reach his goals. Nothing had ever wiggled through even a crack to take his focus from *farm, farm, farm.* There was no way to articulate why this woman was the person who made him forget.

The biggest part of the problem was that when she was in his sight, he didn't care. He didn't care why or how she was in his life, he only cared about touching her. All rational thought died, and he was left with . . . D.

"Good evening, C. Fancy seeing you here." She grinned up at him and it was odd that after only few short encounters he could discern that despite the flirtatious greeting and the easy smile, something wasn't quite right with her.

"Rough day?"

She turned her back on Gallagher's and linked her fingers with his just as they'd done yesterday when he'd come over.

"Yes, actually. It was not a particularly fun one."

She didn't say anything more after that, and though he was tempted to ask her what had gone wrong, there was an invisible line between D and Dinah, between the woman he was having sex with and the woman who worked for Gallagher's and wanted to buy his land.

Her job had to do with his job, in a weird kind of way. Asking about work brought Dinah Gallagher into the equation, and that's not who they were supposed to be in the dark.

"It's so weird working with your family. You think you know what they feel and you think you're on the same page, and it turns out that you're not." She frowned, glancing sideways at him. "It's weird for me to talk about work, isn't it?"

"Weird? I don't know. Complicated, definitely."

She nodded, her eyebrows still all scrunched together.

"But if you *want* to talk about it, you can."

"It isn't anything that has to do with you, really. It's just, Kayla's always the one I talk to about stuff like this. She's my best friend and my cousin and we were always on the same page, and suddenly she just wants to give up."

"Give up what?" He wasn't sure he asked because he cared about what Dinah was upset about, or because maybe this meant her cousin didn't want his land. But if Dinah ended up telling him something that could help him, how could that possibly be his fault? He wasn't taking advantage. *She* was offering. So why did he feel so uncomfortably guilty?

"She wants to leave Gallagher's. My uncle—her father—took over when my father left under . . . less than ideal circumstances. Craig Gallagher is not a particularly nice man, nor one who is too interested in the health of Gallagher's, unless it equals the health of his pocketbook or, more likely, his ego." She stopped briefly, pulling her hand away from his. "We shouldn't be talking about this," she muttered, returning to her breakneck pace toward his house.

"You don't have to tell me," he returned gently, irritated with himself for *feeling* gentle.

"Craig is crazy for thinking I'll let him take my spot, and Kayla is crazy for thinking she should give up," Dinah continued, and Carter could tell she was in her own little world, wrapped up in whatever had wound her up today. "How could she stop fighting? This was our fight. She won't fight anymore, and I don't get it. How could she just *give up* on us having Gallagher's?"

What she said was uncomfortably close to his experiences. His entire life he'd wondered why no one would stand and fight with him. Which he shouldn't share with her, but that was all a long time ago. What did it matter if he told her? "Do you have any siblings?"

"No."

"I have three sisters."

"Three?" She glanced up at him as they approached his gate. "You seem so . . ."

He knew what she was going to say. Alone. Isolated. Because that's exactly what he was. "My oldest sister moved to Minnesota when she got married. The younger two went in opposite directions—California, New York, and my New York sister took my dad with her. Everyone left."

They stopped at his gate and she rested her hand against the post, frowning. "Except you."

"Except me. I've been fighting for something of ours my whole life, and losing because I don't have any power, but it's never shaken my resolve. At least not enough to make me give up. But no matter how much my family loved the farm too, except maybe my oldest sister, no one loved it enough to hold on."

"Did you ever figure out why?"

Carter shrugged. "My sister in California works at a flower farm. My sister in New York went in with Dad on a whole new farm, using what they got for selling our family farm here. I never understood how . . . how it could be the same anywhere else, if it wasn't *our* dirt. I didn't have to turn this place into my own little farm." He gestured at all he'd built, the yard full-to-brim with plants and produce. "But it was the only earth in this whole world that meant something, that my ancestors walked on and tilled and planted things in—even if it was a little kitchen garden. I guess they loved the work, and I loved the land. But as for why?" He shook his head because this was all so damn personal. It was downright friendly, or relationshippy, sharing pasts and troubles.

But he wanted to.

He unlocked his gate and ushered her inside his yard. Instead of leading up to the walk though, he led her around back.

The sun had completely set, but it was a clear night where the stars had started to shine and the moon was bright above. It was a nice night to sit out among the plants and . . .

He paused for a second when he realized he'd been about to think it was a nice night to *talk*. Because for all the sexmails he and D had exchanged, they had also talked about their lives and their problems.

They'd never gone into detail, but they *had* expressed their challenges. So much so he had the fleeting thought that she might have inadvertently told him something in those old emails that might help him in his battle with Gallagher's.

Jordan's words about fighting dirty came back to him, and he frowned. He didn't like it. Not the guilt it made him feel, and certainly not the idea she might have unknowingly given him the ammunition to hurt her.

But maybe he'd done the same. Maybe he'd given her the ammunition to hurt him. It wouldn't hurt to check, it wouldn't hurt to *look*. As much as he enjoyed Dinah—D—whoever they wanted to pretend they were, she would never come before this place. Never.

He weaved his way through the rows of plants to the little slab of concrete that served as his back porch. It was surrounded by an arbor that he grew his blackberries against, making it a mass of vines.

He loved sitting here in the summer when the blackberries were ripe and he could just reach over and eat a few, but it was nice in the fall too, with the nights cool, surrounded by his handiwork.

He guided her to a lawn chair he kept in the back for nights when he liked to sit out under the stars and remember his old life. The old farm. The old days. She sat and he pulled a chair he kept for the random visitor, usually Jordan or Jordan's grandmother, next to her.

"It strikes me that we actually have a lot in common. We just happen to be on opposite sides of things," Dinah said.

"In my experience, people on opposite sides of an argument usually have a lot in common—a lot of the same experiences, and a lot of the same feelings. But because people want different things and need different things, sometimes you find yourself alone, with a farm in the middle of St. Louis instead of where you wanted it to be."

"You don't want to be here?"

"Don't read into that, Dinah." He thought about correcting the Dinah to D, but he waited for her to do it instead. She didn't.

Everything was getting mixed together, though. Talking about land and what they wanted. What they were fighting for. It was all blurring the cross purposes that stood between them.

They sat in silence for a little while, both looking up at the stars and enjoying the way the night air was cooling off after an unseasonably warm September day.

Carter couldn't help but feel a certain sense of loss that spending personal time together wasn't possible long-term. Because no matter how often he told himself it was crazy to have developed feelings for the woman he was exchanging emails with, he had. It had been a fantasy, but that fantasy had been truthful, in that he'd given his honest self to it.

He'd been maybe a better, more adventurous version of himself in the emails, but it was still *him* at the core. Based on the past few interactions with Dinah, he was starting to believe that she'd been herself too.

Unfortunately, she was someone he could understand and admire. Even though she was fighting him, he got why. Much like when his father had decided to sell the farm, he had understood. He'd disagreed with Dad's decision, but he'd understood why Dad didn't have it in him to keep it.

The farm was a struggle, and the price had been exorbitant, and Dad had missed Mom. The farm had gotten so much harder for Dad after Mom died, and even though Carter had done everything to help out, just as his sisters had done everything they could to help, it hadn't been the same for Dad. He hadn't been able to face those memories, especially when so much money was on the table. Dad had figured that farming was changing enough he would've lost it anyway to suburban sprawl, so why not lose it when it still had value?

Carter had understood all of that in his rational, reasonable mind, but his heart had felt completely different. He'd known his mother would've wanted him to follow his heart. So he'd fought Dad and the girls and lost. He hadn't had the power.

Dinah was dealing with a similar struggle. No, she wasn't in danger of losing Gallagher's. It would always be there, and it would always have her name on it. But she was fighting for her place in it, and even though he could never sacrifice his land, it didn't mean he didn't understand.

Since he was twelve years old, he'd understood life is complicated and getting what you want isn't the same thing as being happy. He'd learned very quickly that right and wrong aren't black and white.

He thought perhaps Dinah had that black-and-white view of life. He doubted she'd be able to hang on to that simple view given all of the complexities life could offer.

"You want a drink?" he asked, needing to move away from his thoughts.

"As long as it's alcoholic," she returned with a smile.

He dropped a soft kiss on her head, feeling protective. "I wouldn't dream of anything but."

# Chapter 9

Dinah sat on Carter's little back porch enjoying the cool fall evening and the twinkling stars and moon above.

A light shone from the window of Carter's kitchen, casting flickering shadows on the porch. It was a nice moment. Oddly comforting and warm. It felt like the right thing to do after a bad day. Unwind in this postage stamp of towering plants, the smell of earth overtaking the usual smell of the city.

Despite the fact that nothing could make her not think about Kayla, this was comforting and relaxing as much as anything could be. Even more so when Carter came out and handed her a glass of wine.

"It's some two-buck-chuck shit. I'm guessing a little different than you're used to."

"Long as it gets the job done." She took a sip of the bittersweet liquid. Not the tastiest wine she'd ever had, but she wasn't joking: As long as it got the job done, taste didn't matter.

She slipped off her heels and let them clatter to the cement below. She drew her legs up under her, and she settled in. Because she wasn't Dinah right now, she was D. A woman with no worries and no concerns and certainly no obnoxious family members trying to drive her insane.

Erasing the people she loved from her thoughts, even temporarily, offered little comfort.

She blew out a breath, needing to get out of her head, so she turned to him. Focused in on Carter Trask. Well, C. Or maybe both. "How did you start the farm?"

Carter had settled himself into an uncomfortable-looking chair, and he let out a breath and then took a drink from a can of beer before he answered. "Well, I'd moved in with my uncle on his farm after

Dad sold out. A few years later, he was making plans to sell his place in north county. About the same time, Grandma started falling a lot. She was thinking of selling the house and moving into one of those assisted living type apartments." He paused, clearly remembering his grandmother and feeling sad about it. So Dinah let the silence linger, paying attention instead to the odd sounds of insects in the middle of the city at night.

He took another couple of sips and a deep breath before he spoke again.

"I had a decision to make. I could either move to New York with my Dad and my sister, or I could go to California, where my other sister could probably get me a job. Without my uncle's farm, I didn't have a job or a place to live, and I didn't know what I could do. Farming was the only thing I'd ever done or wanted to do."

This time when he paused, Dinah did something she knew she shouldn't. She slid her hand over his arm. So they were sitting there, chairs next to each other, staring out at the night sky, touching.

Maybe even commiserating, which wasn't supposed to be part of the fantasy—but why not?

"So Grandma, knowing that, asked if I would come live with her as a sort of caretaker. I could work at her restaurant as a busboy or dishwasher and take care of her. Make sure she was taking care of herself. I couldn't imagine leaving St. Louis, I don't know why, so I took her up on it.

"She had this little garden back here for herbs and a few vegetables in the summer. She told me to take it over and do whatever I wanted. Year by year, it just kept getting bigger and bigger and bigger. Farmers' markets started to make a comeback, and I slowly started taking fewer and fewer shifts at the restaurant, and more and more farmers' market booths."

He'd gone from sad and wistful to something closer to happy, or maybe satisfied and proud.

"My next-door neighbor's grandson was about my age, and he worked at the charter school. We came up with an idea for a summer program. It was a slow process, but once I realized I could do all the things I'd done on the farm on this tiny patch of land, I never looked back. This was what I was going to build and keep."

It was quite the story, really, but something about the word *restaurant* stuck there, digging into her brain the way things always did when she had a business idea. There was something there. Fuzzy at first, but it would snowball.

"Did you ever supply your grandmother's restaurant with food?" She studied her wine instead of him, because she wanted her thoughts to move organically. She didn't want to be thinking this *for* him.

"When it was feasible. They had a very set menu they didn't want to change, so they couldn't fool around with what was in season. But when it worked out that I had what they needed, I'd sell it to them, until Grandma sold the restaurant."

That was it. That was what they needed. Not to pave over this beautiful place, but to do something with it. Something connected to Gallagher's.

She opened her mouth to tell him, but then she stopped. No, she had to work out some possibilities and some details first. Talk to Kayla. Talk to the food manager. Make sure this snowballing idea would work, would be as perfect as she thought it could be.

"It must be very rewarding to have built this yourself," she forced herself to say, trying to keep the excitement out of her voice.

Carter shrugged. "I'm not going to lie—it's nice, but I would have preferred to keep Dad's farm. Still, it's not terrible to see how this place has grown because of me."

"There's something to be said for having done it on your own," she said as she watched him take in the entire backyard, his smile growing. "Being able to make all your own choices, put your own mark on it. Don't you think?"

"Yeah, it's not half bad."

"I envy you a little bit. It's hard to make a difference in something that already exists. Settled so tight into history and family, it's hard to make a ripple."

"I'm sure you put an indelible mark on Gallagher's, Dinah. And just about everything else you touch."

It didn't escape her notice he mentioned both Gallagher's and her actual name without backtracking or stopping himself. She thought about asking him if he'd noticed, but she decided to keep that to herself too.

If she could turn this little idea into a big idea, and if she could get everyone to agree . . . it would be possible for them to be Carter and Dinah instead of C and D.

She pressed a hand to her stomach where nerves were jangling ridiculously. Was that what she really wanted? To try to make a fantasy a reality?

She didn't have a great answer for that. She slid a glance at him, all shadows and dark hair in the evening light. He was so handsome and she thought they understood each other really, really well.

She was getting so far ahead of herself it wasn't even funny. She'd gotten better at recognizing when she was diving headfirst into a possibly shallow pool, and though she still didn't always figure out how to rein it all in, she'd figured out how to keep some of it to herself.

She would keep this to herself until she was sure she could make it happen, and until she was sure she *wanted* it to happen.

But then he glanced over at her and smiled, putting the beer can aside. When he slid out of his chair and turned to face her with a delicious, predatory gleam in his eye, she figured tonight she could set those thoughts aside and focus on the here and now.

Fantasy. C and D and the chemistry they had. Tomorrow, during work hours, she would figure out what exactly she could do.

"Did you eat tonight?"

"I did. But I didn't have dessert," she returned with a saucy grin.

He chuckled, kneeling at her feet. His big, strong, rugged hands rested on her knees and he drew his thumbs back and forth across the top. She reached out and combed her fingers through his curly, unruly hair.

Her chest ached and felt all expanded. It almost hurt, even as the shiver of excitement and something else worked its way through her body.

The very bottom line was, she'd never really felt like this with a guy. Being with a guy required letting your guard down a certain amount, and Dinah had been very bad at that part. But it came so easily with Carter. It was like her guard wasn't just down, it had never existed. She supposed that stemmed from how they'd "met."

"Carter," she murmured.

"C," he corrected, his voice deeper and gruffer than it had been when he'd been telling her about building this place.

"Right. C." She studied his face and tried to decide what she needed to say. She'd spent so much time the past week convincing herself this was a fantasy, but it felt oddly real. Comforting and good.

*And you're going to put your whole business and life on the line for some guy?* No way. Gallaghers did not behave in such a fashion. Well, her father did, but she wasn't going to be like him. But she wouldn't be like Craig either, and she wasn't sure she wanted to be like Grandmother. So who did that leave? Who could she be like?

"You okay?" he asked gently.

"Yeah. Yeah, more than okay." Even though it was a lie, she leaned forward and pressed her mouth to his. Her thoughts weren't all right, but this moment was. This man was. So she was going to enjoy it. And smile until she figured out the rest.

Carter had never made out with a woman in his backyard before. Hell, he'd never even brought a woman back here before. It'd been sacred and, granted his grandmother had lived with him for a few years here, but still.

He kept his personal life very much out of this . . . Whatever the farm was. Professional life, blood and soul. But Dinah . . . D . . . She'd snuck under all those usual compartments without his even realizing it.

He'd shoved her skirt up to her hips and was sinking his finger into the hot, wet heat of her body. She sighed against his ear and thoughts didn't matter. All that mattered was sex. Pleasure.

*Dinah*, his mind whispered.

He told his mind to shut the fuck up.

He focused on D's heavy breathing, on the way her fingernails sank into his back. The way she moved against him and the way she pulsed around him. He closed his mouth over her breast, ignoring the fabric in his way. With enough nibbling he found the peak and grinned against her when she squeaked.

"God, I love all the noises you make."

Maybe he shouldn't have said that, but there was a lot to be said for doing this in person rather than over the computer. The feel of her, the sounds she made, the *reality* of it all.

*The connection.* Another thought he told his mind to ignore.

She was practically bucking against him, making those noises over and over again, and he was so hard his cock hurt, and he needed to be inside her so badly he thought he might forget about everything else in his life if he could just have *her.*

"Inside."

She groaned in frustration when he pulled his fingers out of her pussy. "Cruel not finishing me off," she panted.

He grinned at her. "I know. You didn't beg."

She narrowed her eyes at him, but she got to her feet and was quickly heading into his house. "I hope you know, I beg for very little."

"You begged me this morning."

"Exactly," she said regally, stepping into the warm light of his kitchen. "I do not beg twice in one day." She turned to face him, cocking her head in a considering fashion. "In fact, I think it's your turn to beg."

"Baby, I felt how wet you are. I think you're a little bit more desperate than I am."

She fisted her hands on her hips and arched an eyebrow. Though she was frowning at him, he could tell she was repressing a smile beneath it. "I think it's a well-documented fact that women don't need sex as much as men do." Her gaze dropped to his erection. "And trust me, *baby*, you're hardly un-desperate."

"This old thing? I've been taking care of him myself for quite a while."

Something in her expression changed in a way he couldn't read. He'd expected her to laugh or roll her eyes; instead her tongue traced her upper lip and he watched it very closely, taking far too much enjoyment in the moisture it left behind.

"Taking care of yourself?" she murmured.

"I wasn't exactly walking around with blue balls after one of your emails."

Still all regal, elegant, in-charge grace, Dinah crossed her arms over her chest. "Show me."

"Show you?"

"I'd like to see firsthand what you were doing to yourself when you were writing about fucking me." She sank her teeth into her bottom lip as if to suppress a grin, but it failed because she was smiling broadly at him. Something like a dirty challenge in her eyes, which meant he couldn't back down.

And even if he'd much rather have her hands, her mouth, and definitely her pussy on his cock, his hand would do. So, he unbuttoned his pants and unzipped them, watching her as she focused on every moment with intense concentration.

He gripped himself at the base and slowly tugged upward. Dinah made an odd breathy kind of noise. "Turnabout is fair play. I'd like a few images of my own."

She rolled her eyes, but after a few seconds of what seemed like—not embarrassment, exactly, but maybe concern—she gave a little shrug and unzipped the side of her skirt and pushed it down. She looked around the kitchen, and then stepped out of her skirt and her underwear and hoisted herself up onto the counter, spreading her legs so that he could see everything.

"You're so fucking gorgeous," he breathed, because he couldn't keep it in. The way she washed over him like some kind of tidal wave that erased everything except *feeling*.

Her cheeks turned a little pink at that, which was somehow endearing. He really needed to get his shit together.

She nodded toward the erection in his hands. "Keep going."

So he did as he was told, stroking himself slowly, agonizingly, and watching as she trailed her fingertips up her inner thighs. He stroked himself and watched every light move of her fingers, her index finger slowly pressing to the very center of her. She traced that luscious seam, opening herself up to him so he could see everything she was doing to herself.

He was panting now, stroking faster than was probably wise. But the faster and harder he stroked himself, the deeper and harder she pushed her fingers into her gleaming, delicious pussy.

"Don't you dare come by your own hand," she ordered between gasping breaths.

"Right back at you," he managed. "But we better get in the bedroom to get one of those condoms now if we're going to accomplish that."

She nodded and hopped off the counter. They all but sprinted to the bedroom, and he fumbled as quickly as he could to rid himself of his jeans and get the condom on at the same time. She stripped off her shirt and bra and then pulled his shirt off of him once he had the condom on.

"I want you on your back," she said, pushing him onto the bed.

He grinned at her, letting the shove move him to the mattress. "The one place I don't mind a bossy woman."

She slapped him playfully across the shoulder, but took no extra time to guide his cock into her. They both groaned, and he gripped her hips, pushing himself as deep as he could go.

Everything about her was hot and wet and ready, and she didn't play around. She rode him fast and hard. He thrust upward to meet every movement of her body.

Carter thought he might actually be seeing stars. "Come on, baby, I can't last much longer."

She rode him harder, her body practically a blur of movement, her gorgeous breasts moving in time, and everything about her slicked with sweat and need. The lightning-hot flash of pleasure was ricocheting through him so fast, so deep, he released one hand from her hip and managed to work it between them as she continued to slide against him, all frenzied, frantic pace.

He used his finger to push against her, even as he drove into her. She moaned loud and low, thrusting herself against him one last time. He could feel her pussy clench against his cock and he came on a groan of his own.

She collapsed against him, their chests heaving together, their warm bodies slick with sweat.

"Well, Carter, looks like neither of us needed to beg," she said, still breathing heavily.

Using his real name. He should correct her. He should make sure the line was clear, but he didn't have the energy, and with her sprawled on top of him, still pulsing around him, he didn't want to think about other personalities right now.

He just wanted to hold her. Keep her exactly where she was, and he'd worry about that much, much later.

# Chapter 10

The next morning when Dinah woke up in Carter's bed, she didn't feel quite as weird about it as she had the morning before. Still a *little* weird, but she was also coming to grips with the fact that there was something special between them.

Now, reality meant that anything special might still not work out, but she woke up filled with the determination to try to figure all this out.

Why shouldn't she leave her mark on Gallagher's, find a way for Carter to save his farm *and* help Gallagher's, *and* have some amazingly hot sex and good, comforting conversation too?

She'd worked hard her whole life, and though it hadn't all gone perfectly, it had gotten her here. If she put in a little bit more work, a little bit more *grit*, she could have everything she wanted.

She had to believe that, because if she didn't . . . what was there to work so hard for?

She slid out of bed, finding her clothes folded somewhat haphazardly on Carter's dresser. The room itself was haphazard. None of the furniture matched, and while it wasn't exactly *messy*, it certainly wasn't neat. It was cluttered, but it suited him.

Carter reminded her of an artist. His mind was filled with *farm* like some people's minds were filled with *art*, and there was very little room left for anything else in his life.

She smiled a little at that, because she was *all* order and focus, and maybe she was a little bit of what Carter might need.

She got dressed and had to roll her eyes at herself a bit. She believed in optimism, wholeheartedly, but even she was getting a little too optimistic about her idea.

"One step at a time," she told herself, stepping outside the bedroom when she was completely dressed. She still needed her shoes, and would head back to her apartment for a shower and change of clothes. Based on the amount of light coming through the windows, she thought she must have slept later than she had yesterday morning.

She stopped in the small hallway as the smell of something surprising hit her.

Coffee.

She padded into the kitchen, and though it was empty—Carter was surely out working in his little fields—there was the strangest sight on the stovetop. Something she might not have recognized if not for the smell emanating from it.

It looked kind of like a teapot, but rustier and taller. Still, the smell coming from it was definitely coffee.

Which he said he didn't drink, which meant he'd bought and made some just for her. She blinked at the odd little pot and tried to breathe through the tightness in her chest. He'd gotten something he didn't like but knew she did, and she tried to think of the last time someone had done something selflessly kind for her.

It wasn't a big gesture, but it felt big and it hit her hard, and she was disgusted with herself for feeling a little teary. It was just coffee. At most, he'd gone to the store and bought a little bag or can. Why should that touch her?

Because it meant he listened, and thought, and *did*. A combination she didn't know if she'd ever encountered in a guy before, which probably said a lot more about the people she knew than it said about Carter.

Hesitantly, she stepped toward the stovetop. There was a mug with a little note balanced on top.

*Coffee is cheap, but might do the trick. Sugar in the pantry, milk in the fridge. Feel free to drink all.—C*

Dinah swallowed and looked around furtively before she slipped the note into her pocket. She had a lot of emails from the man, but this was handwritten, and it was . . . sweet. Really, really sweet.

She *really* needed to get her head together.

The screen door to the back screeched open and Carter stepped inside the kitchen. "Good, you found the coffee."

His hands were wet, as though he'd washed them before he'd come inside, and yet they were still stained with dirt. Around his fingernails, in the grooves of his skin. He even had a smudge of it on his forehead under the brim of his baseball cap.

His dark eyes studied her and she didn't know what he was looking for. She found she didn't know how to act around him this morning, what with the coffee and the possible ideas for him and Gallagher's rolling around in her head. With *reality* a possibility.

"Um. Yes. Thank you. You don't know how much I appreciate that," she managed, turning from him and focusing on pouring herself some coffee. She had to find D, and all that effortless flirtatious charm that came out when she was around C.

Who'd bought and made her coffee. Of his own volition. Yeah, she'd need at least this full cup to find some sense of calm over that.

She stood with her back to him, staring at the inky brown liquid. It looked to be a little weaker than she preferred, but how could she care? He'd made her coffee. No one made her coffee.

*Seriously, you'd think he'd showered you with millions. Calm it down.*

"So, what farm business have you been up to this morning?"

She could hear him moving around the kitchen behind her, but she wasn't quite steady enough to watch him yet.

"Spraying down the pumpkins with some mold killer. Harvested a butt-load of zucchini. Some broccoli and beans. Market day tonight over in Maplewood."

She took a breath and turned to face him. He was pulling slices of bread out of a bag. "Toast?" he asked, holding up a piece of bread. "I've got some jelly my neighbor made out of my blackberries."

"You're quite the pioneer, aren't you?"

He smiled, and it didn't have that sexy, predatory edge his smiles normally did. It was just a sleepy, morning smile and her heart pinched. She probably needed to get the hell out of here.

"As I opt for indoor plumbing and electricity, pioneer doesn't seem quite apt." Since she'd nodded her assent on the toast situation, he placed the bread into the toaster and pushed the handle down.

She sipped her coffee and considered the rumpled farmer before her. Farmer, of all damn things. "I might stop by the market tonight."

Something in his body froze, almost. Certainly stiffened or stilled. He was silent for too many seconds and Dinah couldn't help but wonder if she'd said something wrong. Maybe he didn't want so much of her time.

*You shouldn't want so much of his.*

Finally his eyes met hers, eyebrows furrowed, mouth grim and serious. "As D or Dinah Gallagher?"

Dinah shifted on her feet. Fair question, but that didn't mean she particularly liked it. Because she didn't know. Dinah Gallagher *should* visit other farmers' markets. It might even help crystallize her idea on how to keep Carter's farm in one piece.

Which was a D thing, most certainly.

"Look, things are getting a little . . . blurry," Carter said, the gentleness in his tone doing nothing to assuage the roiling conflict inside her gut.

"We need to keep these lines clear," he continued, staring at the toaster instead of her. "You know that as well as I do."

Unless . . . But she didn't want to offer him that *unless*. Not until it was a certainty, and maybe not even until she was sure she wanted an *unless*.

*He bought and made you coffee.* Yes, but he was still part enemy, part stranger. Part friend, part . . . more. Bottom line, she wasn't sure of much of anything Carter related, and that made her uncomfortable. Surety had always been her strong suit.

So, she forced herself to find some surety, or at least fake it really, really hard. "I'll let you know what I decide."

She could tell he didn't like the answer, but he didn't say anything else. She kept drinking her coffee, he made toast, and they ate breakfast together as though it was normal.

It wasn't normal in the least little bit, but it was nice. It was comfortable, even with the whole D-versus-Dinah and C-versus-Carter issues.

She decided then and there she would have a real answer for him by the end of this week. That was her deadline, and she always met her deadlines.

Carter was used to working farmers' markets without anyone he actually knew ever coming up to visit him. Which was probably at least partly why he'd been weird when Dinah had suggested she might stop by.

Of course, it was far more complicated than that, but what the hell wasn't these days?

When Jordan showed up at his booth though, Carter could only look at his friend with confusion. "Hey, man. What are you doing here?"

Jordan smiled amiably. "Just thought I'd drop by."

"You never come to the farmers' market. I've seen you shudder and then rail for thirty minutes about hipster nonsense at the mere mention of one."

"Well, they are hipster nonsense," Jordan replied, and his friendly smile was quickly dying. "But Grandma mentioned you had a woman over this morning."

Carter blinked at his friend, surprised, confused, and then a little bit more confused at the odd note of accusation in Jordan's tone. "I didn't realize my sex life had anything to do with you."

"I didn't realize your sex life had anything to do with Dinah Gallagher."

Carter didn't have anything to say to that; probably couldn't have managed a word, the way his breath seemed to leave him.

"That's not exactly what I had in mind when I suggested fighting dirty."

Carter bit back the nasty things he wanted to say. Things that would probably prove a few points he didn't want proved. "It's not fighting dirty. I don't know what your grandma told you, but it's none of your business."

"Because you're going to sell, aren't you? Because of a pair of tits."

Carter ground his teeth together to keep from reaching across his table and possibly punching his friend. Which was a strange reaction. He'd never been a particularly jealous guy, and he'd definitely never been a violent guy. But anyone talking about Dinah that way... Damn it, he was screwed up. But that didn't mean Jordan had any right to talk about this.

"What are you doing here? I told you I'm not going to sell, and I'm not going to. I don't need to fight dirty to do it, and my sex life is completely and utterly separate from anything to do with selling."

"No, it's not. Certainly not if you're fucking Dinah Gallagher."

"Listen . . ." Except Carter didn't know what to say. The guy was worried that if he sold his farm, it would hurt Jordan's grandmother, and Carter got that. In Jordan's situation, he'd be worried too, but he couldn't imagine going to the guy's place of business and interrogating him about his romantic entanglements. Fuck, had he really just thought the term *romantic entanglements*?

"You want to buy something or you want to interrogate me? Because this is my place of business, so an interrogation will have to wait."

"I was pretty surprised to hear it, Carter. I thought we were friends."

"We are friends, and this has nothing to do with my business, or your grandmother's house, or being friends. Who I sleep with has nothing to do with you. It has nothing to do with my land, and it has nothing to do with your grandmother."

"My grandmother is just trying to keep her house."

"So am I!"

Jordan shook his head, arms crossed over his chest. "This is un-fucking-believable, you know that, right?"

He opened his mouth to tell Jordan to leave, except he realized that Jordan wasn't looking at him. Possibly not even talking to him. He was looking across the way, and when Carter followed his gaze, it landed right on Dinah Gallagher.

Fuck.

"You can go now," Carter ground out.

"I'm not going anywhere. I have a little something to say to Dinah Gallagher."

"Don't. If you're really my friend, I don't need your help on this."

"I thought we were friends, and now I think you're really just screwing over us all."

"My land isn't going anywhere and neither is your grandmother's." The anger bubbling inside of Carter wasn't proportionate to the situation, but this wasn't exactly new either. When people befriended you because of a cause, the friendship rarely lasted. Because at some point, that *cause* was going to drive you apart.

"I've been used enough in my life to know what that feels like, so if this is about friendship, I'd tone down the neighborhood and land talk. And if you have anything to say, I suggest you say it to me before she gets over here."

"Because of course she's coming over here."

Carter squared off with Jordan, feeling both angry and irritated, and a little guilty. He didn't know how to handle those conflicting feelings. Because he'd always pursued his causes to the end of the earth, and he'd never had to stop and wonder if he'd faltered.

But Jordan was making him question his cause, his life, his *guilt*.

Dinah approached his booth in her Gallagher's business best. A floral skirt that skimmed her hips and went to her knees, high heels that showed off her slender calves and the red color she'd painted her toes, all with a matching silky blouse, and brightly painted lips.

No matter that things were weird and complicated and that Jordan was standing there staring daggers at both of them, Carter just wanted to sink into that gorgeous mouth and think about nothing else.

But everything else was right here. All around him.

"Good evening, Dinah."

"Good evening, Mr. Trask. I don't want to interrupt. Feel free to finish with your customer before you talk to me."

"Dinah, you remember Jordan."

"Oh, right! The charter school teacher." She smiled brightly at Jordan. "It's good to see you again."

"I'm also a Washington," Jordan said, his tone flat.

Dinah's eyebrows drew together and she looked at him questioningly. "A Washington?"

"Mila Washington is my grandmother. Your father tried to, you know, con her out of her house so you guys can expand."

"You mean my uncle," Dinah returned, her business smile still in place, though it tightened.

"That make it better for me?" Jordan said.

Dinah's smile didn't waver, but it did change. "I'm sorry if my uncle wasn't as kind as he should have been, but I assure you, Gallagher's has nothing but the best interests of the neighborhood at heart. And it seems as though you've retained your land. No harm, no foul."

"Barely, and only because I stepped in when she told me Gallagher's was intimidating her. You guys like intimidating elderly women? Well, we're not going to let you do it. We're not going to let you ruin this neighborhood and turn it into some white-bread, suburban bullshit. This neighborhood is real, and we're not going to let you guys come in here and suck the life out of it."

"Mr. Washington, Gallagher's has been here for over a century. We're just as much a part of this neighborhood as anyone. All we want to do is bring in more revenue and more—"

"Fuck your revenue," Jordan spat.

Carter couldn't take it any longer. No matter that Dinah could handle it; he couldn't sit here and let . . . Well, he just couldn't. "Jordan, come on. You don't have to be an ass."

"Nice side of the street you're walking on these days. See you later, man." Then Jordan strode away.

"I'm sorry," Dinah said, frowning after Jordan's retreating form. "Did I cause a problem with you and your friend?"

"No. I caused that problem."

Dinah was quiet a few seconds. "When you hooked up with me, you mean."

He couldn't read her tone, and he found he didn't want to. He rubbed his fingers on his temples to alleviate the headache that was now pounding there. "Why are you here, Dinah? I assume it is Dinah business, right?"

"Yes. Dinah Gallagher, who would very much appreciate if Carter Trask would meet me at a neutral location for a business meeting after your market."

"Dinah." He shook his head. "I'm not selling. What could there possibly be to talk about?"

"It's not about selling. It's about a new, alternate option."

"There are no new alternate options. There is only *I keep my land*, and Gallagher's does not get it. Nothing can change that."

"What if this business proposition includes a stipulation that you keep your land?"

Carter's head pounded harder at that nonsensical statement. "You said you have to get my land in order to make your mark or whatever, so I don't see how—"

"Please." She reached across his table, giving his arm a squeeze. "Just meet me. You can pick the location, and the time, and we will sit down and have a business meeting. And, if you say no, I will take no for an answer and never bring it up again."

"You'll never bring it up again?" he asked suspiciously.

"Not *this* idea. I'll still try to buy your land if you refuse this deal, but I'll leave this business proposition completely off the table if you say no." She thrust out her hand. "Deal?"

The last thing he wanted tonight was a business dinner with Dinah. He was feeling confused and guilty and pissed off, and her in her business demeanor only served to piss him off further. But the quicker he agreed, the quicker he could tell her no and move on.

He took her hand and shook. "I'll meet you at Capilierries at eight, okay?"

"Capilierries at eight. I'll be there." She shook his hand and smiled, and he didn't have the energy for the tightness in his chest or the want in his gut. He didn't have the energy for the complication of Dinah Gallagher.

But he had the complication, and he couldn't seem to work up the decision to give it the old heave-ho.

She glanced down at his table of produce and selected a watermelon. "And I want to buy this."

"Five bucks."

She only grinned at him. "A steal." She handed him a five-dollar bill before sauntering off the way she'd come.

This was nothing but trouble and it would only serve to irritate him, so why he was smiling as he watched her sashay away he would never understand.

# Chapter 11

Dinah sat at a tiny table in a hole-in-the-wall Italian restaurant she'd never eaten in before, and waited for Carter to show. She was nervous, for a lot of reasons. Considering it was now ten after eight, she was a little worried he wasn't going to show up.

Would that be the end of it? He'd just stand her up and ... then what?

She shook her head, sipping the glass of water in front of her and trying to remember she was Dinah Gallagher, future director of operations of Gallagher's Tap Room. She was not some lovelorn email correspondent who'd be devastated if all this didn't work out.

When Carter finally pushed through the restaurant door, she let out a sigh of relief. It didn't eradicate the nerves, since she had a whole slew of them, but at least he was here.

He was here and she could lay out her plan and ... he would say yes. He would have to say yes, wouldn't he? What would be the benefit to saying no? Even if he wanted nothing to do with a real relationship between Dinah and Carter, this was *still* in his best interest.

*Is it in mine?*

That scary question kept popping up in her head, and she kept pushing it away. Of course it was. This idea was genius. Kayla hadn't gotten excited about it, but Kayla was having her own weird thing.

Carter slid into the seat across from her, an almost-smile on his face. Yeah, he was not helping her nerves at all.

"So, do we have to do the dinner thing or can we just get this over with?"

Yeah, definitely not helping with the nerves. "If that's what you want, we can do it that way. I'll cut straight to the chase." And hopefully not lose her lunch in the process.

Before she could get any more words out, the waiter appeared. Carter smiled at him, though it was still that tight, lackluster curve. Even when he turned it on her. "You know, why don't we order some dessert? They have really great cannoli here, if you like it."

"Okay. Yeah, that'd be great. Maybe a bottle of wine too. Whatever dry red you've got on hand."

Carter shifted uncomfortably as the waiter left, but she could see there was a certain struggle going on with him. He was here, and he didn't want to be here, but at the same time he'd showed up and ordered the cannoli. He'd agreed to meet her. So whatever was happening, he was just as conflicted as she was.

Which was a helpful reminder. One that allowed her to calm down a little bit.

"Right. So cut to the chase on this whole business thing?"

Dinah gave a sharp nod. "The fact of the matter is, neither Kayla nor I were particularly one hundred percent behind Craig's idea to buy out the three lots behind Gallagher's and turn them into a parking lot and a farmers' market. But we were both very into the idea of hosting our own farmers' market, especially in this neighborhood and with our locally brewed beer available." She could tell he was losing interest word by word, second by second.

She tried not to panic, because she *never* panicked when it came to business. She was always smooth and in charge. She couldn't lose it now just because a guy she . . . cared about, somewhat, was involved.

What kind of businesswoman would she be then? "I ran my idea by Kayla and our head chef at Gallagher's, and I think I have a way to involve you in our plans without buying your land."

"I'm not trying to be a dick here, but I don't need to be involved with Gallagher's. I'm not selling, period, so I don't *need* a compromise. I do just fine on my own."

"You could do better. It would bring us both added revenue. Because I think a lot of people are very into the local food movement right now, and if you became a food supplier, we could develop a small, but completely local menu. It would be a serious draw and solve both our problems."

"But I don't have a problem. I was never going to sell to you."

Dinah swallowed down her frustrated comments and snarky retorts. Sure, he hadn't planned to sell to her, and she knew how much the land meant to him. So, yes, it probably would've been quite the climb to get him to sell, but she wasn't ready to concede the point that he might have sold to her if she'd found the right leverage.

But she didn't want to find any kind of leverage. She just wanted to have things work. She wanted to help Gallagher's in a way Uncle Craig couldn't argue with. He couldn't argue that this wasn't a much better use of their money and connection with the community. Even if he didn't agree, the board would surely outvote him.

A farmers' market would cost so much money to start, and working with Carter wouldn't take very much at all: a new menu, and most of the food costs would simply be diverted from the food budget they already had.

Carter was a stubborn man, suspicious after having been burned a lot. She needed to find some patience with him. He probably deserved a little bit of patience.

He'd bought her coffee. He'd made it. He was a man worth . . . well, something.

"Are you saying that you sell every piece of produce every season at a few farmers' markets? Wouldn't it be easier to work as a partner with a restaurant that would—"

"Get to dictate what I grew, and when they wanted it, and what quality it had to be. A partner who would have a say in everything I do on a day-to-day basis. A partner who could pull out at any time, leaving me with nothing. Is that the kind of partner you mean?"

"Obviously there would be a contract, and—"

"A contract that would benefit Gallagher's far more than it benefited me. Even if I could afford a lawyer, I can't afford one like yours. Any contract would be stacked against me from the start."

Dinah couldn't believe he was still arguing with her. It had been a perfect solution. How could he not see that?

"Dinah, I know you're trying to do the right thing here."

His estimation she was *trying* to do something right only made her bristle further. She had every right to buy his land, too. This was not about doing the right thing, it was about compromise. Help. Working together.

"I don't trust the Gallaghers. I don't trust them to have my best interest at heart, or even be equally invested in my interests."

"I am part of Gallagher's," Dinah replied, trying to keep the emotion out of her voice.

"You want me to trust you, but I don't have any reason to."

It shouldn't hurt. His not trusting her shouldn't have any effect on her whatsoever. What right did she have to think he should trust her?

But it did hurt her feelings and she was surprised to find she even felt a little teary. Which was obnoxious and embarrassing.

"I'm sorry," Carter said gravely.

His apology somehow made it worse. He probably only felt bad because she was sitting there looking all too close to tears. His *sorry* had no real regret behind it. What on earth was wrong with her thinking she could . . . could . . .

"I do wish things could be different," he said softly, and it was the first gentle thing he'd said that didn't piss her off. Because she wished that too. If they both wished things could be different . . .

"Don't you think if we both feel that way, there's something we could do about it?" she asked, trying not to sound desperate, even though she was afraid that's exactly what she was being.

"I've spent my life not getting what I wanted. Sometimes there isn't anything you can do about it."

She reached across the table and put her hand on his. It was warm and strong, but he had been beaten down a number of times. Maybe he needed someone to stand up and fight with him, like Kayla had always done for her before this week. "Sometimes, Carter, there *is* something you can do about it. Sometimes there are options and chances and possibilities if you're willing to fight a little bit."

"Baby, I have done nothing but fight my whole life, and I'm tired of it. I've got what I want, and I'm not going to lose it." He turned his hand and curled his fingers with hers, giving a little squeeze.

It hurt to see the failed fights right there in his eyes, but not the way things normally hurt. Not because it affected her in any way. She hurt *for* him, and she wished he could have had something go his way.

"What is the worst thing this could do to you?" Dinah asked. No matter how she hurt for him, she wasn't willing to back down. "It's not like it would break you. If you set some of the terms and you still had your farmers' markets, you'd still have the income you have now. You'd just be adding to it."

"It isn't feasible."

"You don't know yet! You haven't even considered it. I won't ask you to make a decision right now, but I am asking you to think about it. Maybe come up with a plan where you think it could work, and then I can look at it and see if it works with what I have in mind. Don't you think it's worth a shot to at least *consider*?"

What she was really asking was, didn't he think *they* had a shot. She knew it was dangerous to ask with her heart, when her brain needed to be in charge of business.

Letting herself do this was an anomaly, and she almost told him how she never mixed business and her personal life, but that would give him too much power. It would certainly show him just how pathetic she was.

"All I ask is that you think about it," she said resolutely, trying to focus on the business side of her brain. "Think about a possible way it would work for you. If you can't find a way and we can't work anything out, then we move on. But I think it has a chance to be really great, and I would love for you to consider it. Please."

He stared at her for a few seconds, lines bracketing his mouth and his forehead. So serious and world-weary for a man who couldn't be too many years older than her.

When he finally spoke, he looked down at his hands. "Why?"

She blinked and sat back, trying to take a calm breath instead of a sharp inhale. She knew what he was asking. It wasn't just your average why, it was why not keep fighting for his land? Why not take him down in the way she was so sure she could?

Which meant her answer would have to be honest, and that scared her more than anything. To be honest and to show her weakness to him. But she liked him. Really liked him.

She liked him enough to come up with this alternative plan. Enough to want . . . more. When had she ever been scared of going after more?

"I don't want to buy your farm, Carter. I will keep pressing you on that if it's the only option. Paving over the place would give me no pleasure and no joy and I don't think it's in the best interest of Gallagher's." She shouldn't have said that, but it came pouring out of her. She'd never had feelings like this before, and she didn't know how to compartmentalize them the way she usually did.

"If it's all I can do to get my rightful place, I will do it. But, if there's another way, I will find another way."

"So . . . this has nothing to do with D and C?"

She could say it had nothing to do with that. She could lie, and she had no doubt she could make him believe that lie. But she didn't want to lie about it. Not to him. Not now.

"I wouldn't say it has *nothing* to do with . . ." She could've said *them*, kept up this farce that D and C were separate from Dinah and Carter. But the whole point of this meeting was that she didn't want to keep up the farce and the war. She didn't want to pretend. She wanted to be Dinah with him, and she wanted him to be Carter. She wanted them to work together and see what could grow.

She wanted reality. Which was frightening, and she'd never been a fan of things she didn't know how to conquer. But she wasn't a coward, even if she was afraid.

"It is partially about *us*," she said forcefully, letting it sit there between them like the little bomb that it was.

Carter could not in a million years have predicted this. There was certainly nothing he could have done to prepare himself for this compromise, this offer . . .

*It is partially about us.* She had said that as though she felt everything he'd been feeling the past few days. As though she felt strongly enough to want to change the course of her business plan.

He didn't know what to do with that. Not as the waiter put the bottle of wine on the table. Not as he put the plate of cannoli between them. Nothing about the romantic scene in the little Italian restaurant, with the beautiful woman across the table from him, made any sense whatsoever.

He studied Dinah as she took a seemingly careless sip of wine before sliding a cannoli onto her plate. Anyone who walked past her would think she was completely and utterly unaffected. A woman on a date having a decent enough time, maybe a little bored.

But he saw the flicker of nerves in her hazel eyes, and the way she nibbled on the cannoli rather than actually eat it proved his point. She wasn't suggesting this on a whim. Or because the sex had been amazing. She felt the same things he felt and she was willing to put some of her pride on the line for it.

He admired that about her, even as it scared the living hell out of him. What was he supposed to do with this woman? She was beautiful and nearly perfect and far too smart for his own good. If he agreed to this, what else would he agree to?

It felt like a slippery slope, and God knew Jordan and the rest of the neighborhood would judge him for partnering up with Gallagher's.

But he hadn't been lying to Dinah when he'd said he was tired of fighting. He was tired of standing up for his land and always having to protect it and struggle for it. A partnership with Gallagher's would at least put off the fight for a while.

As much as he was growing to care for Dinah, against his will, he still couldn't imagine a scenario where he gave up this farm he'd worked so hard for.

"I can't promise anything, but I guess I could . . . consider it."

She set her wine down a little bit too hard and her grin spread so bright and so fast he couldn't fight the bolt of pleasure it gave him to bring her some semblance of happiness.

"You'll really think about it?"

"*Think* being the operative word. I'll have to put together some thoughts and plans, look at finances and all sorts of things of that nature."

"Absolutely. And if you have any questions or anything you want me to ask our chef, I can get you any information you need. I really think this could be great. For Gallagher's and for you and . . ." She trailed off as she frowned at her wineglass.

"And for us?" he finished for her, because he had no doubt that's where her thoughts were going.

She glanced up at him, eyes serious. "Yes. Us." She took a deep breath. "I think *us* could be . . . good. Don't you?"

It was insane, but he did think that. How it had come about made no sense, and actually finding a way around her uncle trying to buy his land, it all felt so surreal.

But she was here, across from him, gorgeous and real and wanting the same things he wanted. Wanting to fight—not against him, but with him. How could he not think it had all the potential in the world for *good*?

So he smiled. "Yeah, I do."

# Chapter 12

"I followed you last night."

Dinah stopped in her tracks in the hallway of Gallagher's. Though she'd never been fond of her uncle, his tone and his words were downright creepy, enough to have her shivering.

She turned slowly to face him, trying to maintain an aura of not giving a fuck. "That's certainly a creepy statement, *Uncle* Craig."

"A man wouldn't have to be *creepy* if his family members weren't a bunch of lying, cheating deviants."

Dinah tried to fight off the shudder of fear, but it got the better of her. *Condescending* Craig she'd always disliked; flat-out *hateful* Craig actually scared her a little bit.

"You know, fucking the enemy doesn't make you any more moral, and certainly not any smarter than your father."

"You *spied* on me?" she asked, rage replacing revulsion so quickly it nearly made her sway. "Who the hell do you think you are?"

"The director of operations of Gallagher's, who will be damned if I let a slut ruin everything I've worked for."

"You have *some* nerve."

"You are supposed to be buying Carter Trask's land, but instead I find you—"

"I have no interest in hearing what you *found* me doing," Dinah returned, cold and angry and disgusted that he would go to such lengths. She couldn't even be worried about how it would affect her deal with Carter, she was so outraged.

"I'll be bringing this to the board."

Dinah lifted her chin. "Go right ahead. I have a few things to bring to the board myself."

A muscle ticked in Craig's jaw as he narrowed his eyes at her. "Like what?"

Interesting. He very nearly sounded concerned. "I guess you'll have to attend the meeting tomorrow and find out for yourself."

"Watch your back, Dinah," Craig muttered, stalking off in the opposite direction.

Dinah let out a shuddery breath. Though her uncle could be mean and intimidating, she'd never felt scared in his presence before. She didn't care for it, especially when she would need to move Carter along on his decision now. She couldn't let Friday's board meeting pass without bringing up her suggestion.

She closed her eyes and turned into Kayla's office. Craig knew about her and Carter. Which shouldn't be a terribly big deal, but it would be. It made her look bad. It made her look stupid. It made her look young and foolish and everything the board already thought of her.

"Fuck, fuck, fuck."

"So, it's true."

Dinah nearly jumped a foot when she realized Kayla was actually *in* her office, sitting behind her desk, looking pale and tired in a way that immediately worried Dinah. "Hey, are you all ri—"

"Are you really sleeping with him?"

Dinah blinked, surprised by the undertone of hurt in Kayla's voice. "I . . . Kay, he . . . he's the guy. The . . . the email guy."

Kayla shook her head, her expression scrunching up. "What do you mean?"

"I mean, Carter is the guy I've been emailing. I mean, I didn't know that until . . . Well. It's not . . ." Dinah blew out a breath. She hadn't thought about actually explaining this to her family. She really hadn't thought about much.

The realization she'd lost sight of quite a few things since figuring out Carter and C were one and the same made it hard to catch a full breath. She was a planner, but she hadn't planned this whole thing out at all.

"Why didn't you *tell* me?"

Dinah tried to come up with an answer to that question. Kayla was her best friend and usually they told each other everything, but Dinah hadn't wanted to tell anyone about this. Especially when it had all happened so fast and out of the blue and . . .

"I was sitting there, going to meetings with you to convince him to sell his land, and you were sleeping with him? You didn't think I should have some clue that was going on, considering everything we were up against?"

"It wasn't going on the whole time. It hasn't even been going on that long. I just . . . happened to put all the pieces together that he just *happened* to be the guy I'd been . . . emailing. I know it's a little crazy, but it's true. So, I didn't know how to . . ."

"Didn't know how to tell me he was the guy you'd been emailing? Didn't know how to tell me this man we were supposed to *crush*, was someone you started sleeping with? And now you've got this insane idea to fold this guy into our business *after* you slept with him? This isn't like you, Dinah, and it's messed up."

"Look, I know it looks a little odd, but I promise it isn't messed up in the least. You know I would never let anything come before Gallagher's."

"I don't know that, actually."

"Kayla!"

"I'm sorry, did you learn *nothing* from what your father did?"

Dinah felt as if she'd been slapped. Those words were certainly the metaphorical equivalent, and coming from Kayla . . . "That was hardly business, Kayla. I resent the implication—"

"You're right. Not business. It was just my mom. My family. That's all. Hardly important."

Dinah stepped toward her cousin, anger mixing with some of the hurt. "You know I do not condone anything my father did. You *know* I'm just as furious at him for doing that to my mother as I am that he did it to your father, regardless of my feelings toward Craig. I don't know how you could possibly compare me to him. I know something is going on with you, but turning it around on me is unfair and just plain mean."

Kayla shook her head. "I don't like this. I don't like thinking that you're being . . ."

"That I'm being what?"

"You're either being fooled by this farmer guy, fooled by yourself, or maybe just blinded by your damn ambition. Not long ago you were determined you were going to buy his land. No matter *what*. How many times did you tell me that? Then you find out he was the creepy guy you were creepy emailing and—"

"He's not creepy. It was never creepy. A little out there maybe, but not creepy." Why she was bothering to defend herself on this point was beyond her, but it seemed imperative. Hell, if she couldn't convince Kayla everything was normal, she wouldn't convince a damn board member.

"It seems creepy to me. You don't know him. He doesn't know you. I don't know how you could possibly think this is a good idea."

Dinah swallowed the lump in her throat. This was not what she had planned, that was for sure. She wasn't sure how to deal with business stuff and emotional stuff all mixed up together. She didn't know how to face her cousin, her best friend, sitting there telling her that everything she was doing was wrong.

Kayla had always backed her up. Always agreed and supported, and Dinah didn't know how to feel except betrayed. "So, I take it you won't stand with me at the board meeting," she managed to say, though her voice was tight and scratchy.

"No, I won't. Because I think you're making a huge mistake, and because I quit."

"I know you think you want to—"

"No, Dinah, you don't understand. This morning I told Dad, Grandmother, and the board that I quit. Effective immediately. I won't be a part of Gallagher's anymore. I don't want to do this anymore, so I'm not going to. I can't wait around for the perfect job. I have to get out of here and find some semblance of sanity. It's not you, and it's not my dad. I can't be a part of this anymore."

"So you're abandoning Gallagher's. You're abandoning me." Which probably wasn't fair, but that's what it felt like. Their whole lives they had planned to take all this on, and now she was backing out. Quitting.

"I don't think you'll miss me, since you don't tell me anything anyway."

"I would have told you."

"Yeah? When?"

Dinah didn't have a good answer for that. She didn't have an answer for any of this. It felt like her father leaving all over again. It felt like . . . She didn't know. Things kept changing and people kept leaving. Everything that Gallagher's was supposed to be was going all wrong, and no matter how hard she tried to fight it, everything seemed to unravel.

Kayla stood up, and that was when Dinah realized she'd been packing a box of things from her office.

"I'm sure I'll see you around. If I'm allowed at family gatherings. Grandmother was pretty angry."

"So we're just...done. Not friends anymore. Not partners. Just 'maybe I'll see you at a family gathering'?" Dinah's mouth wavered and tears threatened, but she fought them back with everything she had.

Kayla paused her uncharacteristic outburst, and Dinah held her breath. Surely Kayla would see this was all wrong. How on earth could she be quitting?

"You know what? I can't do this now."

"So you quit, and you leave, and you run away. How very brave of you, Kayla," Dinah threw at her, because she didn't know how to be hurt without pretending she wasn't, but her pretending was failing her.

"I've never been brave, Dinah. If I ever have a chance of being that, I have to get out of Gallagher's and . . ."

"And what?"

"And you. I'm sorry, but I have followed you around like a puppy and let you tell me what's right and . . . I have to figure out who I am. Not who you want me to be." With that, Kayla sidestepped her and walked right out of the office.

Dinah could only stand, frozen. She felt unjustly accused and angry and sad and hurt and a whole slew of things she didn't have the emotional capacity to unravel.

She forced herself to take a breath and then another. She would not cry at work. She would not break down at work. She never had before, and she wouldn't start now. Kayla was having a personal crisis and she needed some space. Well, Dinah would give it to her for once.

Maybe Kayla was even right. Maybe they both needed a break from each other.

The tears threatened harder but Dinah blinked them away and focused on Gallagher's, because that was the thing that stood the test of time. People? Not so much. But a name and a place? Absolutely.

Kayla could think Dinah's idea was a mistake, but Dinah *knew* the deal with Carter was a good idea for all of them. She wouldn't be deterred from her conviction. She would sit down and she would work on a presentation for the board, even if Carter hadn't agreed yet.

He would. He had to. He had to understand this was the best thing for all of them—Gallagher's, and her and him, and even Kayla and Craig, damn it. The board would understand. Her idea made business sense, and the board wouldn't let personal bullshit cloud their vision.

She would have the future she had planned for herself from the time she could remember. Dinah running Gallagher's. Dinah in charge, making her mark, and damn happy doing it.

She stomped around Kayla's desk and sat down in Kayla's chair, ready to focus and get right to work on her proposal.

Instead, she buried her head in her hands and cried.

Carter had been restless for three days straight and it was starting to drive him a little crazy. On the plus side, he had certainly done enough work for three men. Plants were weeded, picked, packaged, watered, and he'd even made some random repairs that he'd been putting off around the house.

Now he was grilling dinner for what he assumed would be Dinah's impending arrival. Without discussing much about schedules or the like, they'd gotten into the habit of having dinner together.

Dinah talked business and supplier ideas, and Carter mainly fed her and distracted her with sex. Dinah seemed to be energized by talking about business, but for Carter this was a decision he'd needed to make in quiet and in his own time.

So, he'd let her prattle on without talking much himself. All in all, it had begun to feel very domestic and . . . real.

Which was downright scary as hell. He didn't have a clue as to what he was doing, and he didn't have anyone to talk to about it.

His friends weren't the kind of friends you talked to about women or identity crises or whatever the hell he was having. He'd discussed the business portion of his issues with his family, but he hadn't mentioned the complication of Dinah and Gallagher's, and relationships. His sisters would just start talking about marriage and settling down and missing the whole damn point.

So he was left to fumble around trying to figure out the right thing to do when it came to the infuriating woman he couldn't get out of his head.

The thing was, Dinah had tapped into something he had wanted to do for a while. He'd gotten a little taste of the possibilities of being someone's local produce supplier a few years back, but Grandma's restaurant had never fully gotten on board with that.

Someone actually developing a menu around what he grew? It was a hard thing not to get really excited about.

He didn't trust Gallagher's. He wasn't even 100 percent certain he trusted Dinah. Gallagher's would always come first for her. His farm would always come first for him, so he understood that. He didn't even want to change that about her, but he didn't know how to safeguard himself against the damage that Gallagher's could inflict.

His youngest sister had hooked him up with a possible lawyer, and though he couldn't afford it, his family had rallied around the idea, offering what they could. If he wanted to do this, he had support. Even from thousands of miles away, his family had his back on this.

*Finally.*

"Something smells delicious."

He glanced over his shoulder to where Dinah was walking through his rows of beans. She was wearing a skirt and impossibly high heels, and how he had fallen for such a put-together, business-type woman was completely beyond him.

But he had fallen for her. Pretty damn hard.

"Thought I'd grill tonight."

She walked up next to him and hovered there. He glanced at her face, noticing that something was off. He couldn't quite put his finger on what, and maybe she was just feeling awkward because he hadn't agreed to anything yet, but there was a strange lack of energy from her.

"You know a girl could get used to not having to cook for herself. Although I have the sneaking suspicion that under that lid you probably have just as many vegetables as you do pieces of meat."

"My evil plan uncovered."

She smiled at him, something a little wistful in her expression. So he reached out and touched a strand of hair that was curling around her cheek.

"Rough day?"

"Very," she said emphatically.

"I suppose if we're going to be business partners, you could probably tell me about it, if you wanted to get it off your chest."

She reached out and grabbed his arms, her eyes wide and a smile hovering at her mouth. "Does that mean you're going to agree?"

There was so much hope in her expression that even if he'd been about to say no, he wasn't sure he could've said it. Which was certainly scary, to know she had that kind of power over him. No one had ever had that kind of power over him.

He'd fought his family, the people he loved, every step of the way for everything he had, and knowing he might not fight her . . .

Damn.

But here he was, and he didn't know how to go back. Reversing had never been something he'd managed to do. He was all plowing ahead, forward motion, pounding against the world until something worked in his favor.

Why should this be any different? "If we can agree on some terms, then I don't think it would be a terrible idea."

She flung her arms around his neck, nearly knocking him into the grill. Her grip around him was so tight she practically squeezed the breath out of him.

"You don't know how much I needed to hear this tonight," she said, her voice a little rough. "This is fantastic." She pulled back, a broad smile on her face, but something nearly manic in her expression.

She started pacing in front of him like some sort of whirling dervish. "This is going to work. I know it's going to work, and it's going to really be great for everybody. I promise you, I will not let you down." She grabbed his arms again, squeezing. "You will not regret saying yes. I promise. I promise."

"Baby, you can't promise that. That's all beyond your control."

She looked at him with a kind of horror in her expression that didn't fit the situation.

"Things might not work out, but we'll give it a try. You don't need to promise things. We'll give it a shot."

"Things are going to work out. I believe that with my whole heart." She covered her heart with both her hands and he wanted to reach out and soothe some of this overly serious earnestness.

He opened his mouth to argue with her before realizing it was futile. Maybe she needed to believe everything would work out. One of those optimists. He should probably let her keep that delusion.

"There's a board meeting on tomorrow night. I think the best course of action is to work on a presentation to give them. Together. Work on it together. Present it together."

It was his turn to step back in horror. "Board meeting? Me at a board meeting?"

"You should be the one to present the safeguards you want. We should work together to come up with a presentation, fine-tune what we're each going to say, but I don't want to speak *for* you. I think it's important we're separate entities."

He grimaced. Dinah had a point about the separate entities thing, but the absolute last thing he wanted was to be in a boardroom full of Gallaghers.

"It's not going to be easy," she said somewhat cautiously, wringing her hands.

He wasn't sure he'd ever seen such a nervous gesture from her before. "What's not going to be easy?"

"My uncle, Craig Gallagher, the director of operations, he, um, knows about us."

"About . . . us?"

"He followed me at some point and worked out that we've been . . ." She shook her head. "I can't believe he did it, and it's gross and creepy that he did, but the bottom line is he knows we've been involved, and he's made it very clear he'll use it against me."

"Which will make the board question your judgment on me as supplier."

She stiffened considerably and he was sorry to have said something that clearly hit a sore spot. But it was also clearly true. "We don't know what they'll think, and we won't know their opinion on the business matter until we've presented this to them. It's such a good idea."

"Not all good ideas come to fruition."

"It will. This one will. It has to. Carter, I . . ." She took a deep breath, back to pacing, back to un-Dinah-like behavior after un-Dinah-like behavior. "Kayla was always my ally," she said softly. "She always had my back, and she quit."

"Over this?" he asked incredulously. Jesus H, the last thing he wanted was to get deep into Gallagher-family crap.

"No," Dinah replied firmly. "She's having her own weird thing. Hell, half the Gallaghers are having their own weird thing." She shook her head before straightening her shoulders and quelling her nervous hands. She met his gaze fiercely. "We are definitely going to be up against some opposition, but we have right on our side. We have the best interests of Gallagher's on our side. There's no reason not to do it, I just wanted you to know so you're prepared."

She crossed the distance between them, curling her fingers around his forearms. "Don't change your mind. Please, don't change your mind. I can see the wheels turning." She gave his arms a squeeze, her expression imploring. "I just need someone to stick with me on this. Because I know that it's the *right* thing."

He wanted to tell her no. He wanted to put the kibosh on the whole stupid idea. What were they thinking? This idea was idiotic and probably going to bite them both in the ass, and yet she looked at him with those big hazel eyes and clear desperation. He couldn't say no to her. He couldn't run away from someone who needed him to stand up with her. He'd been there. He had felt that desperate need for someone—anyone—to stand with him, to fight by his side.

"I'm not going to back out," he said.

She squeezed him into another hug. "Thank you. I promise—"

"On one condition."

She pulled back a fraction, cocking her head. "Condition?"

"You have to stop promising me things, Dinah. You can't make promises in business. We don't know what will happen in the board-room, and God knows, me in a boardroom is a scary enough prospect on its own, let alone if people know we're sleeping together. But it's business, and I know part of this is so we can be Carter and Dinah, together."

She stepped back a little bit as if she was uncomfortable with his admission, but it was true. The only reason she'd come up with this plan, and the only reason he was agreeing to it, was because they had feelings for each other.

"Even with that being the case, we have to draw a little bit of a line between what happens with Gallagher's and what happens with us. Every business I've been a part of has included people I love." He almost immediately regretted using the word *love*, so he kept steam-rolling on, hoping there were no meaningful pauses in there. "I've had to fight my family and disagree and argue, and it sucks. I don't want to fight with you, if we're going to do this. I don't want busi-ness crap to become a part of *us*."

"But . . . I thought the whole point was so we could combine our lives as who we are, and I am Gallagher's."

"I'm not quite sure what the whole point is, but I know I need a little bit of distance between what's going to happen in that boardroom and who you are here."

"It's the same person. Dinah in the boardroom. Dinah in the bedroom. That's . . . the whole point."

"You really think Dinah Gallagher is the same as D?" Because he didn't. He'd met both, spoken to both, understood both. D was more of the truth underneath all those things she was so certain she *had* to be.

Hell, he knew it because he'd used C for very similar purposes. To be someone he didn't know how to be in real life.

"I'm not D. She was a little fantasy I indulged when I had time. In reality, right here and now, I am a Gallagher. My business means everything to me."

"If you were happy with that, you wouldn't have needed D. You can't argue with me. I did the same thing. I was drowning in my own life, so I created this other one. But it was me. If it wasn't honest, we wouldn't be here . . . having feelings for each other."

She wasn't looking at him now, her face all scrunched and so not the powerhouse woman she usually was. He felt like shit for undermining any of her confidence, but he had no idea how to get through to her that there was a danger in her thinking she was Dinah Gallagher and nothing of the woman he'd gotten to know in emails. In sex. In the past few days. Words, at least spoken ones, had never been his strong suit.

"Let's pause and eat. Maybe talk a little bit about what you want this presentation to be."

"And not fight?" she asked, sounding very weary.

"I'm tired of fighting, remember?"

"I don't want to fight either."

"Let's enjoy dinner. Then we'll talk business, and then . . ." He forced himself to smile at her, trailing off.

"And then?" she replied, some of her spark returning.

He grinned. "Dessert."

# Chapter 13

Carter served her a delicious dinner of grilled local pork chops and—not quite, but almost as delicious—corn and beans. He'd bought her a nice bottle of wine and poured her a glass with dinner while he drank from a can of beer.

She had never been in a relationship like this. Where the guy did really nice things for her without her ever having to drop hints. Where they could talk about their jobs and be interested in each other's families and memories. She didn't know if it was because they shared a similar passion for businesses rooted in their family histories, or because their personalities simply made it easy for them to talk.

All Dinah knew was she really, really enjoyed him. She'd been able to relax after her shit day and their odd conversation.

It was important that the board meeting go well, and even more important that she live up to the promise she'd made Carter: that this would work out and be good both for his farm and for Gallagher's. He could say he didn't want promises, but ensuring this idea's success was of paramount importance.

If they worked together, if they planned everything out, they would succeed. They would have to succeed. "All right. We're done eating. Now we discuss business."

He leaned back in the little chair on his porch. They'd eaten outside in the cool fall evening, and Dinah couldn't express how much she enjoyed these little moments. Outside. Stars. Meals together.

*Business, Dinah. Focus.*

"You sure you don't want to skip to dessert?"

"Unless you're referring to an actual brownie and not a euphemism for sex, no. I want to focus on business first."

He pushed out of his chair, still grinning. She thought of her first impression of him, all scowly and grumpy, the enemy. But there was so much under that rough and gruff exterior.

"Sit tight," he murmured. He disappeared into the kitchen, and when he returned he had a pie. "You like cherry?"

"Yes. That looks store-bought, and here I thought you were Mister Local, twenty-four-seven."

"They're made and distributed by a baker in New Benton."

"Where on earth is New Benton?"

"Far away from the city, Gallagher, but it still falls within the hundred-mile designation for local foods, so I maintain my twenty-four-seven reputation."

She chuckled as he cut her a slice of pie, and that was when she noticed he also had a file folder under his arm.

"Dessert *and* business? Those might be my two favorite things."

"I hope to amend those two tops later tonight."

She laughed and reached out her hands, making a grabby-fingers gesture. "Give me the folder."

"Hold your horses." He kept the folder firmly tucked under his arm as he sliced himself a piece of pie and slid it onto a plate. Taking his sweet time, he sat back down in the chair across from her and placed the folder firmly out of her reach.

"These notes aren't for you, it's just my chicken scratch so I don't forget anything. Nothing formal. Just my terms. I talked to my sister, and there's a lawyer she knows in California who is willing to look over any contract we negotiate."

"Can you afford a lawyer?" She realized a little too late she'd offended him by asking that question. But he'd been the one to mention it the other day.

"I'll handle what I can afford. You just make sure Gallagher's is being fair."

"All right. Tell me your terms."

Carter went through the assurances he wanted and the things he could promise in a contract. Dinah asked questions and tried to analyze it from what she knew of menus and cost and supplies. She'd need to set up a meeting with Simone, Gallagher's head chef, before they went to the board. She'd need to ensure that Simone was on board and that all the details were ironed out.

"And that concludes the business portion of this evening." He flipped his folder shut and narrowed his eyes at her. "Don't you dare argue with me."

"As much as I love business, I suppose I could be encouraged to set it aside for the remainder of the evening. We can continue our conversation tomorrow after I've talked with our head chef."

Something flickered across his expression, possibly uncertainty or something very close to it. She opened her mouth to promise him things would be great, and then she remembered he'd told her not to promise anymore. It was hard not to. Hard not to assure him she could take this on and she could win. Very few people put their faith in her, and she *had* to live up to the promises—even if they were only promises in her head.

"Let's go for a walk."

"A walk? All I have are heels."

"Just around the farm."

He held out his hand and she took it, letting him pull her up from the chair. "Around the farm, huh?" Since *the farm* was a yard, it seemed like an odd request, but she went along with it anyway.

"Sometimes it's nice to walk around in the semi-fresh air and look at the stars and listen to the sounds of the night."

"Sirens and car doors slamming and—"

"One of these days I'm going to take you to the country and see how well you like it, city girl."

Dinah pretended to shudder at the idea of the country. "All that open space and lack of Starbucks?"

He rolled his eyes and shook his head, but he held her hand as they walked through the rows of plants. Even though the space was small, there *was* something nice and refreshing about walking around on a starry night, seeing all the things he grew. Leaves gilded moon-silver and fruits sparkling. It felt like magic.

*He* felt like magic. She couldn't believe it was a magic she got to take part in.

He stopped their progress in a little corner at the side of the house. He reached out and brushed some hair out of her face. Something inside of her shivered in time with goose bumps popping up on her arms.

He had a sweetness and tenderness about him she not only wasn't used to in men but didn't quite know how to accept or reciprocate. All those sweet little gestures made her throat close up and nerves flutter around in her chest. She couldn't remember being very nervous with guys. Not really; certainly not like this.

"You're very beautiful all the time, but especially in the moonlight."

"And you are surprisingly romantic," she managed, though her throat still felt all closed up and tight.

"For a farmer?"

"For a *guy*."

He chuckled at that, still drawing his fingers across her face. She leaned into him, even with the jangle of nerves rushing through her. There was still something so enticing about what he could make her feel, nerves couldn't make her stop.

"Dinah."

"What?"

"I just wanted to say your name. Your actual name."

Her stomach flipped and fluttered, so she reached out and stroked the same pattern across his face that he'd been stroking across hers. Bearded and rough, such a strong, rugged face. "Carter," she murmured.

It was alarming how much she felt. Her heart was jittering, and her breath was ragged. She didn't feel steady or certain of *anything*. It was all too much and too big for something so new and potentially fraught.

But no matter the alarm, it was wonderful to feel this way. Amazing to have someone as invested in the possibility of her, as she was in the possibility of him. She couldn't resist sinking into that feeling and all of the potential that existed between them.

She pressed her mouth to his and let herself be soft and gentle. Which she wasn't sure she'd ever allowed herself to be. She didn't try to take charge, and she didn't try to remember some email exchange they'd made. She just fit her mouth to his and enjoyed the ride.

Carter didn't have the first clue what he was doing. But ever since Dinah Gallagher had walked into his life, uncertainty had become part and parcel. She was this bright, otherworldly creature he didn't know how to resist or control or manage.

So he let himself go, in ways he probably never had in his entire life.

He kissed her like she was the special woman that she was. He didn't think about all the emails they'd written to each other; he didn't even think about the things they'd done to each other in the past few weeks.

He savored the taste of her mouth and the feel of her arms coming around him. He allowed himself to take and give in equal measure and he didn't rush. His mouth cruised over hers as his hands slid up her back. For a few humming, sensual minutes all they did was kiss. Their tongues lightly brushing, their mouths gently touching. There was nothing rushed about it. There was nothing fantasy about it. Because she was Dinah and he was Carter.

His heart beat unsteadily in his chest at that thought, but it still didn't stop him. Because the magic of Dinah was that no matter how many reasonable, sensible things his brain told him, feeling took over. Feeling won.

He tangled his fingers through the silky strands of her hair and angled her head just a pinch so he could slowly, erotically, agonizingly deepen the kiss, millimeter by millimeter. Fraction by fraction.

She made a little sound in the back of her throat, but she didn't push any more than he did, a rarity for both of them when they were together. To stall. To languish. To relax into the enjoyment.

Her palms slid up his back, a possessive grip. She had so many opposing forces inside of her—a strong, iron-like certainty in her life; a soft pliancy in his arms.

"Let's go inside," he whispered across her mouth.

Her lips curved as her eyes fluttered open. "I suppose we've given your neighbors a few too many shows these past few days."

"So far no one's complained." He unwound his hands from her hair, but he wasn't content to lose that touch. He kept his arm around her shoulders as he led her around back and in through the kitchen.

They walked quickly into his bedroom, never stepping away from each other, never breaking contact.

Real. Honest. *Them.* Those words were haunting him a bit. Carter and Dinah, possibly the two people they could least afford to be, and yet how did he not afford this? Her?

He walked into the center of the bedroom, then turned to face her. Her hair was mussed, her makeup kissed off, even her usually impeccable clothes were rumpled. "I like you this way," he murmured, letting his fingers run down the edges of the little blazer-coat thing she wore before he pushed it off her shoulders.

"What way? About to have sex with you?"

"Well, that. In addition to rumpled. Messy." The jacket fell to the floor.

Her lips curved into that little self-satisfied smirk as she trailed her fingers down his chest. "Funny, I wouldn't mind seeing you in a suit. Do you own a suit?"

He narrowed his eyes at her, taking her wrists and wrapping his fingers around them. They were narrow, and he could feel the steady thrum of her pulse. "No business talk," he warned in a low voice.

She pouted, but she didn't try to free her hands from his tight grip. Instead she pushed up onto her toes and pressed her mouth to his.

This time things weren't quite so slow, or gentle, but it was still different. Everything about them today was different, and he enjoyed it far too much, because it was going to hurt like hell eventually.

But eventually wasn't today.

He squeezed her wrists before he released them, and then they were pushing clothes off each other, trying to keep their mouths fused as they did. He nudged her onto the bed, covering her long, soft body with his.

He tasted her everywhere, the sweet wine of her mouth, the soft salty tang of her skin, the musky spice of her pussy. He brought her to orgasm with his mouth, and he rode through said orgasm with a hunger he didn't know how to fulfill.

She was already reaching for the box of condoms as he kissed up her body, and once he was over her again, supporting himself with the shaky strength of his arms, she slowly rolled the condom onto the pulsing hardness of his erection.

They were both shaking with need, gasping for breath, and still neither of them pushed for a quick finish.

She trailed her fingers down his temple, his cheek, and his jaw. Her eyebrows were furrowed as if she was trying to solve some problem or riddle. He knew the feeling; this felt like both, and yet . . .

And yet, here he was. A beautiful, complicated woman underneath him, touching him with a gentleness that surprised him.

Her gaze met his, her expression morphing into a sheepish smile, and though he had doubts about just about everything else, he didn't have doubts that they were feeling the same things: too big, too much, too complicated, and not giving a shit.

He sank into her, her legs wrapping around him, her sigh in his mouth. It didn't make any sense, but deep inside her, connected to her, he didn't care. He moved, agonizingly slow, enjoying the near painful twist of anticipation as her body met his, again and again.

She sighed, she moaned, she moved, and he watched it all, absorbed it all, wanting Dinah imprinted on his body, his memories, his heart.

Shit.

She wrapped her arms around him, coming apart in his arms, his name on her lips. It was that whisper, his name, *her* that culminated in his own rushing release.

They held on to each other as if that was all it would take to solve the million complications that surrounded them. With Dinah in his arms a supportive relationship and business success seemed infinitely possible. Carter figured he could let himself believe in that for a little while.

# Chapter 14

Dinah had a plan. God help anyone who tried to stand in her way. Including the frustrating man in front of her.

A man she was more than a little terrified she'd fallen in love with. Every time that little thought pushed into her head, she shoved it right back out. Because love took time and trust and . . . time.

She tried not to think about how time hadn't helped her parents any, but maybe they'd never loved each other. Or maybe a midlife crisis could eradicate love.

It didn't matter. She wasn't worried about love or her parents, she was worried about the board meeting they were going to be late for if Carter didn't let her dress him.

"I'm a farmer, Dinah. Board meeting or no board meeting, I'm not wearing a fucking suit. Some decent khakis and a polo are good enough to stand there and nod while you deliver the spiel."

"You're going to have to talk. That's why we've been practicing. I'm only giving the opening remarks, you—"

"Yeah, yeah, yeah. I get it." He glared at the tie she'd pulled out of his closet. "I'm still not wearing a fucking suit."

She forced herself not to glare right back at him. She had to be calm and reasonable here. The businesswoman to his . . . little whiny baby.

"Don't you want them to take you seriously?" she asked, working on a compassionate tone instead of an irritated one.

"If they can't take me seriously because of my clothes, they're not going to take me seriously, period."

Dinah let out a sigh, and he flicked a glance at her. One that clearly recognized how irritated she was despite the fact she was trying to hide it.

She forced herself to smile. "I know this isn't your favorite—Oh." It dawned on her then, that he wasn't being difficult to be a dick, or because he was childish—things she'd begun to worry about.

"Oh what?" he growled.

"You're nervous," she returned, true sympathy working through her. She tended to forget not everyone dealt with business presentations routinely, and it might be intimidating.

He glared at her. "No shit."

"You don't have to be nervous," she said, moving toward him. She felt compassionate enough she might even not press the suit issue, though she was a little concerned he could have that kind of influence on her. "I have it all planned out. It's going to go perfectly." She rubbed his shoulders and gave him her brightest, surest smile.

"You aren't nervous at all?" he asked incredulously.

Okay, that probably wasn't quite true, but going into the lion's den meant affecting a certainty, a surety. Any nerves had to be ruthlessly buried in confidence. "I have a sense of purpose, and you should too. We both believe in this proposition, right?"

He took a deep breath and she was almost afraid he'd say no, that he was just doing it for her, which might be the most awful possibility she could consider.

And made it all the more imperative she succeed at convincing the board that working with Carter would be a better alternative than paving his farm over.

"Look, I don't mean to play the woe-is-me card, but like I said, I've wanted a lot of things in my life, but I'm not so used to getting them."

"You never had me on your side."

He chuckled and shook his head. She wanted to give him a reassuring hug. She wanted to press her lips to his. She wanted to tell him . . .

*Focus, Gallagher.*

"I'm not going to do the suit, not because I'm being difficult, but because I won't be able to concentrate on what I have to say if I'm that uncomfortable. Fair?"

She gave a little nod. She didn't like it, but it was fair. To *her* it made more sense to do the uncomfortable thing if it would present a clear, professional image.

Sure, the board would likely expect a farmer to show up in jeans and a dirty T-shirt, and Carter's attempt at business attire was a step up from that. She wanted to prove to every single person on that board there was so much potential in this man.

She knew most of the board members, and they would almost unanimously roll their eyes at a guy who'd plowed over his yard to create a farm, but she needed to show them how genius and right it really was.

There was so much at stake, and she'd always believed that one's appearance, as the first impression, was an important first step to success.

She gave him another once-over with a somewhat critical eye. He'd trimmed his hair and his beard and he looked a little bit more *groomed* than usual. She was surprised to find on a personal level she preferred the wilder, more unkempt look he usually went with. Of course, Carter seemed to be an expert at being the opposite of what she usually found attractive.

She smiled to herself. Even in the suitable khakis and black, non-descript polo shirt, he made her chest ache a little. He was *handsome.* Maybe not slick-businessman handsome, but he had an elemental authenticity to him she couldn't help but admire.

This was going to be fine. They just had to follow the plan and it would be totally, 100 percent fine.

"We should probably head over. I want to get set up before all the board members get there."

"All right."

"You don't have to look quite so much like you're about to walk death row," she said, completely, inexplicably charmed by his reticence.

"I'm presenting a business proposition to a board of Gallaghers who have thus far only sniffed around to buy my land. Trust me when I say, it feels a little bit like I'm a dead man walking."

"I promise, it's not going to be like that."

Carter let out a sigh. "I know this is important to you. I hope you know, for all my arguing and sighing, it's important to me too."

The way he could genuinely cut to the heart of things, to lay his feelings or beliefs on the line like that, it never failed to take her breath away. "I do know that."

"Good. Because I don't have that thing you do, where you can cut it all down to the most important part. I don't know how to do the maneuvering. Sometimes I'm just going to be the unpolished me that I am, and I don't want you to mistake that for not caring."

His gaze was so earnest. Dinah marveled at how serious this had gotten, so fast. So out of the damn blue, but it was here: her heart constricting, her *need* for this to work—the partnership, *them*. "It'll be fine. I prom—"

"Stop."

"I know you said no promises, but—"

"I know you need your certainty, Dinah. I get that, and I'll even try to match it. It's going to be great and everything will work out, but . . ."

"Certainty doesn't have *buts*."

He cracked a smile, but it faded rather quickly. "On the tiniest off-chance that it doesn't work, I need you to understand that's okay."

"How is that okay?" she demanded. He kept saying he understood how important this was, but she was having a hard time believing him.

He took a deep breath and let it out. He shook his head and she knew he didn't have an answer. Just like *she* didn't have an answer. Because if this venture didn't go through, she would still have to work on finding a way to buy his land. No matter how horrible it made her feel, that's what she'd have to do.

Gallagher's was her soul and her life, and nothing was going to change that. Not even possible love-type feelings.

What did romantic love—if that's even what this was—have over centuries of family and roots and importance? What did feelings have over the knowledge and the surety she belonged here—in this neighborhood, making a difference with Gallagher's Tap Room?

"We need to get moving."

"Dinah . . ."

"I know this is what's best for Gallagher's," she said. If she focused on *that*, and not what she might feel for Carter, or what might happen if she failed, she could get through this in one piece.

"So you keep saying."

"I just need you to have half as much certainty as I do," she implored as they made their way to the door.

"I don't know shit about Gallagher's, Dinah. Maybe it would be helpful to them, but maybe it wouldn't."

"What about you? Aren't you certain it'll be helpful to you?"

He sighed. "I think . . . I think it could be good, and I think it could be a challenge that I would really enjoy. But it isn't necessary, and the more you make it seem necessary, the more uncomfortable I get."

Dinah frowned as they walked out of his house. She tried to come up with a response as he locked the door and they moved toward the gate, but she didn't know how to deal with her certainty causing his uncertainty.

That's where she kept circling back to with the whole feelings-for-him thing. She didn't always agree with him, and she didn't always like what he felt or said or wanted to do.

But no matter how she wondered over it, her *feelings* for Carter dominated. The flutter in her chest, the painful desire to be with him when she wasn't, the way he made her laugh or sigh or just . . . relax.

She couldn't think about love right now. She couldn't think about *Carter* right now. She had to think about Gallagher's, and only Gallagher's. Her entire life had been navigating the weirdness of running a business with family and people she loved. This shouldn't be a new thing, all in all.

In fact, it should be comfortable and old hat. But Carter wasn't like her family. She and Carter didn't have a common good to rally around. She needed Gallagher's to succeed. He needed his farm to succeed. While she had found a way for them to do that together, it wasn't the same as having that same goal.

But as they walked toward Gallagher's, Carter did what he so often did when they were walking together. He took her hand in his, linking their fingers.

She'd never been with someone who was so effortlessly affectionate. Even her family was *so* not that.

Gallagher's loomed in front of them—her home, her heart, and a threatening tower of brick, all in one.

"We'll just go do everything like we practiced," he said, sounding sure for the first time.

She realized clearly in that moment that he said it for her. And for him. It hit her, harder than she'd allowed it to yet, that he was doing this because of her. Just as she had come up with the idea because of him.

She wanted to make this work beyond almost anything else. Which was intimidating and made this whole thing that much more complicated. But she had never been afraid of complication, and she'd never been afraid of a challenge, and she wasn't about to start now.

"We'll blow them away. And when they agree, we'll celebrate in grand fashion."

"Oh, baby, your grand fashion scares the hell out of me."

She laughed because he probably should be scared by her idea of celebrating. They were so different. She didn't understand what it was about him that worked, or even what about her attracted him. All she knew was being with him made things feel comfortable and *right,* even when they weren't.

Now she just had to jump over one more hurdle to make sure she got to keep everything she'd been building with Carter.

Carter wasn't sure what he'd expected exactly. The cozy meeting room with exposed brick walls and comfortable seating had certainly not been it.

There was a big oblong table that people sat around after they filed into the room. Most of the members were older, and definitely dressed in suits. Carter immediately recognized Craig Gallagher, the man who'd so condescendingly tried to buy his land.

He should hate the guy for that, but he found after hearing Dinah talk about him, he was even angrier that Craig Gallagher treated Dinah so poorly. That she had someone in her family who would sabotage her, who would follow her like some kind of creepy stalker.

It wasn't right. He'd had his share of family disagreements, his share of downright awful moments, but his family had always clearly *loved* each other, and supported each other as much as their opposing viewpoints would allow them to. He couldn't imagine anyone in his family purposely hurting him or his chances to do what he wanted to do.

So when Craig Gallagher sneered at him, Carter sneered right back. Dinah's hand rested on his leg under the table. She gave a little squeeze and he knew it was a signal to ignore Craig. She wanted him to put the business face on.

The problem was he had no business face. No poker face whatsoever. When he felt disgust or discomfort, which he felt in equal measure here, it was really hard to mask his expression, but he gave it a shot.

The last person to walk into the meeting room was an older woman. She was so well put together and steady, Carter couldn't quite discern her age beyond much older than everyone else in the room.

Which was when it dawned on him she must be Dinah's oft-spoken-about grandmother, whom Dinah feared and revered in equal measure.

It was surprising how seeing someone else's grandmother could remind him of his own, could hit him with a visceral pang of grief out of the blue.

Once he breathed through it though, it was an odd comfort. His grandmother would have approved of this venture so much. She would've loved it, and so he would renew his efforts at a poker face and succeeding for Grandma as much as for Dinah.

Craig Gallagher opened the meeting with roll call and personnel issues Carter had no interest in whatsoever. He was here for one reason only.

"Dinah, you have a proposition for the board." Dinah's grandmother's voice was crisp and authoritative and Carter couldn't help but fidget a little when that shrewd hazel gaze landed directly on him. He felt as though he was being summed up and wholly found lacking.

"Yes." Dinah pushed back from the chair and stood. "I know Craig has had an idea in place to buy the land around Gallagher's for expanded parking and a brand new neighborhood farmers' market. While we've managed to obtain some of the properties, most of the remaining owners are steadfast in their loyalty to their land. Ms. Mila Washington and Mr. Carter Trask have both flat-out refused to sell."

She was so incredibly smooth. It didn't surprise Carter in the least as she began their spiel. She spoke with authority and confidence and everything about her looked sleek and polished. It was amazing to see. Intimidating, actually. But not too much, because he also knew how to make that woman writhe and beg underneath him, and he thought maybe he knew the real Dinah beyond all of this business stuff, in a way he didn't think her family did.

Oh, they understood her dedication, but he didn't think they understood her passion. She *felt* things, she didn't just do them. That had gotten to him from the beginning. She *believed*. She tried to dress it up as business and family legacy, but the bottom line was, she was a very emotional person.

Dinah turned the presentation over to Simone, the head chef. Carter had had a long discussion with the woman this morning and he liked her. She had a no-nonsense demeanor about her, and she was passionate about ingredients and food. They would likely argue over what he grew, the quality of the produce, but that was the kind of business relationship he wanted. One that was about quality and care, not the bottom line.

Carter noticed that most of the board was rapt. They had listened to Dinah's presentation and now Simone's, but the more the two women spoke, the angrier Craig appeared.

And the more Dinah's grandmother's gaze focused in on Carter.

Once it was his turn to speak, he'd have been lying if he'd said he wasn't sweating a little. Dinah's grandmother was really unnerving him.

He stood as Dinah had instructed in their preparations, and he began his practiced speech.

"It's no secret that I have no great affinity toward Gallagher's. I have been treated poorly at the hands of some of you, and I have been underestimated by I think a lot of you. But I also know how much you love Gallagher's, because this is the same thing that drives me to hang on to my land and my farm. I'm not giving up my piece in this world. There's nothing that Gallagher's could do to make me give up my roots, my family, and my heart."

It didn't escape Carter's notice that Craig snorted and leaned back in his chair, clearly agitated and angry. For some reason, it only spurred Carter on to make this more personal and more honest.

"When Dinah approached me with a compromise that would allow us both to have something that we wanted, and help this neighborhood, I was skeptical. I don't trust a lot of you, and I've been shoved off land by the likes of you people for decades." He was going a little off script, but he thought it was working. Some of the people who'd clearly gotten a little bored had sat up and taken notice again.

"You can't have my land, but I do think we could create an effective partnership. One that would extend your local food and sustainability reach, and one that allows me to keep what I will not give up. I've been selling at farmers' markets for years now, and my farm has grown in profits exponentially. I'm an expert at getting the most out of my yields, and as Simone discussed, working one-on-one together would allow her to create a unique menu that only Gallagher's would have. This is the only way I will work with Gallagher's, and quite frankly, if you say no, it's no skin off my nose."

Dinah nudged him under the table, but for as much as he understood business maneuvering and faking it, he had to be honest. He had to put all of his cards on the table so everyone understood what they were doing here. It was going to be a partnership, not a fiefdom.

"I can tell you, few people take as much pride in their produce as I do. My product is my everything, and I know that's something Gallagher's understands. I think a partnership would be beneficial to both of us. There's just no good reason to say no."

With that, Carter sat down. He felt oddly exhilarated and *right*. That certainty Dinah was always asking him to have, he felt it now. Because they could say no. It didn't matter. He knew it mattered to Dinah, but surely if she felt half of what he did, she would see it really didn't. Not once she got over the shock.

"This kind of endeavor requires a vote."

"Then I move that we have one," Dinah said to her grandmother.

"Very well. Simone, Mr. Trask, Dinah, please leave. Our vote is for board members only. You will be notified of the result at a later time."

"Technically, I am part of the bo—"

"Technically, your vote is noted. Dinah, please step out of the room with your . . . group."

"I have something to say before they leave the room," Craig said with a smirk, standing and carefully buttoning his suit jacket.

Carter felt Dinah tense, almost as much as he did to keep himself from lunging at her bastard uncle.

"As we all know, Dinah comes from a certain kind of genetic material."

"Yes, a Gallagher. Just like you, Craig," Dinah shot back through gritted teeth.

Craig continued as if she hadn't said anything. "We know how dependable her side of the family is. How much we can entrust *that* side with members of the opposite sex."

"I don't know what this has to do with anything, Craig," Dinah's grandmother said sharply. "Sit down."

"Then you must not know, Mother. Because Dinah Gallagher here and Carter Trask have been engaging in a sexual relationship for weeks."

If it surprised Dinah's grandmother, she didn't show it. Based on the way she'd been analyzing him all meeting, Carter would be surprised if she didn't know.

"My personal life has nothing to do with this proposition. You have the facts in front of you in the handouts, and from our presentation. If you want to make this a personal attack, Craig, I think we all know why."

Though she was clearly vibrating with rage, Carter gave Dinah credit for the calm way she spoke.

"My boardroom will not be a soap opera," Dinah's grandmother said, a little bit of anger vibrating within her as well.

"It's my boardroom. I am the director of operations."

"And I gave birth to you, which makes me the only reason you are here. You will sit down and you will listen to me."

Carter could only blink at the way everyone jumped to do Dinah's grandmother's bidding. He could see Dinah there in sixty years or so. In charge, even if she wasn't supposed to be. A leader. The head of all this.

"If the three of you would now exit, we will send someone to give you the verdict once we've reached a conclusion."

Carter was ready to do whatever Dinah asked of him. If she wanted to refuse to leave, if she wanted to confront her uncle, well, he would stand right here with her.

But she graciously and calmly got to her feet. "We'll wait at the bar until you have an answer." With that, she strode out of the office door with her head held high. Simone followed, and Carter walked after her.

"Worthless slut."

Carter whirled around at the murmured words. "What the hell did you just say?"

Craig smirked. "I believe you were told to leave, farmer boy."

"Carter." He looked at Dinah, standing in the doorway and gesturing him toward her. Only that kept him from demanding Craig repeat his childish insult. So he could slam a fist in the smug asshole's face.

"We cannot vote if you do not leave, Mr. Trask."

Carter leveled Dinah's grandmother a look, no longer intimidated by her, from the sheer force of his anger. "Yes, some business meeting." He stalked out into the hallway.

"What in the hell are you doing?" Dinah demanded.

"I'm not going to let him say shit like that about you. Not on your damn life."

"It's just business. You have to let it go."

"Like hell I do." He only kept himself from jerking away from her hand resting on his arm because she probably needed comfort more than she needed his anger. But, damn, he was fucking riled now.

"Carter, calm down. He's . . . he's a bully and he's lashing out." Dinah blew out a heavy breath, her gaze drifting back to the closed meeting room.

"Yeah, clearly I missed some background here."

Simone disappeared into the kitchen. Dinah led him downstairs, winding her way through the somewhat crowded restaurant to a little corner of the bar that was mostly empty this early in the day.

They slid into seats, and he noted Dinah looked exhausted. Back there she'd been a force, but it seemed to have leaked out of her. He took her hand in his, gave it a squeeze.

Her mouth curved, barely, the saddest attempt at a smile he'd ever seen from her. "A couple months ago my father had an affair with Craig's wife. They ran off together and obviously . . ." She looked down at their joined hands, drawing her thumb over the bumps of his knuckles.

He wished he could offer her some other kind of comfort, but he didn't know what to do with that kind of information. That was a pretty huge deal, not that he thought it excused Craig's behavior.

"Craig's never been a great guy. He's always been a little bit of an arrogant prick, and quite frankly, so is my dad. But . . . my dad was in the wrong on this, so a lot of people are cutting Craig a lot of slack. I happen to think he's spiraled out of control, but he lost his wife to his brother, and that's not exactly easy stuff."

"It doesn't explain why he blames you."

"I'm here. I'm in his field of vision. My mom left too, so it's just me here for him to focus his blame on. It might not be right, but it is what it is. If I let it get to me, I lose sight of what I have to do, and I refuse to let that happen. He won't beat me."

"You're allowed to be hurt by what your uncle said to you," Carter said softly, reaching out to brush a finger across her soft cheek. She seemed so certain she had to be this impenetrable force, and he saw how that could break her eventually.

"Now is not the time for this. The vote should be our complete and utter focus."

"Dinah."

"I'm not talking about it anymore. It isn't important. He doesn't know anything about me, Carter. He's nothing. All that matters is they vote yes. That's it."

He covered her hands with his, realizing with a harsh pang of regret she was perilously close to tears. "Take a deep breath."

She jerked her hands away from him, but then she did take a deep breath and closed her eyes. "I'm sorry."

"Baby, you don't have to be sorry about that. Someone in my family said something like that to me? I'd . . . It is not right. It's okay to be pissed."

"No. It is what it is, and I have to accept it. I can't change him. All I can do is take my rightful place. Once they vote yes on this, I'm one step closer to doing it."

"You really think *yes* will solve everything?"

She met his gaze, her hazel eyes watery, but damn if her certainty didn't grow back like a weed—quick and twice as tough. "I know it will."

Carter got a harsh, sinking feeling in his chest. He hadn't realized quite how . . . Well, Dinah had some real issues, and she was very much in denial about them. He didn't know how to deal with denial. He'd never had to fight denial, never had to see it through or prove himself. When his family left, he'd had to start over every time.

He couldn't help wondering if when Dinah finally realized she couldn't power through everything, he'd be left alone to start all over again.

# Chapter 15

Dinah had been fine all day. Calm and in control and certain, but something about Craig's parting shot and Carter's reaction had jumbled her all up and she felt shaky and scared and not at all certain of the outcome.

The longer it took the board to deliberate, the longer and tighter her nerves stretched. The more Carter held her hands and told her to breathe and sweetly called her baby, the more she wanted to scream. Just *scream*.

When Grandmother finally appeared to summon them back, Dinah nearly sobbed with relief. Which was also scary. She couldn't remember the last time she'd felt so emotional.

*Maybe when Dad disappeared? Or Mom decided to move? Or—*

"Dinah, I'd like to see you in my office. Mr. Trask, your presence will not be required."

"Wait. Did the board vote? What's this all about? If they voted no, I—"

"I said I wish to see you in my office, Dinah. We will discuss the rest there." She flicked a glance at Carter. "Mr. Trask, you are dismissed."

"I'm *dismissed*?" Carter asked incredulously, and Dinah had a feeling it was only the way she squeezed his hands that kept him from saying something snarky back to her grandmother.

"Yes. You are," Grandmother said regally, because she was a woman who never backed down from a perceived challenge.

Dinah could tell that Carter wanted to argue with her grandmother, and she could tell he really didn't appreciate the way people were talking to him around here, but his gaze studied her and eventually he just nodded.

"Call if you need anything. Let me know how it goes. I'm not going far." He gave her hands a squeeze before he released them.

She wanted to grab on and hug him. Hold on to Carter and insist he be allowed to come with her, but her grandmother's wanting to talk to her alone was a frightening and confusing prospect. Usually Grandmother was happy to let whatever happened with the board happen. This was unorthodox and problematic.

Carter disappeared and Dinah looked at her grandmother, trying to discern some clue as to what was going on.

But her grandmother's face was blank. Always the unreadable matriarch who held all the power, and Dinah suddenly felt as though she had absolutely none.

From the moment her father had disappeared with Aunt Linda, the power she thought she'd had growing up had been completely eradicated, which meant it was never hers in the first place. It had all been Dad's, and she'd just foolishly thought she shared some of it.

She followed Grandmother up to the older woman's chic, spacious office, feeling oddly beaten. All of her confidence and certainty deserted her.

"Have a seat," Grandmother instructed as they entered.

Dinah took the uncomfortable chair opposite Grandmother's desk while Grandmother sank into her plush leather armchair. Dinah clasped her hands in her lap, desperately trying to find some sense of strength and determination.

"The board has voted in your favor."

Dinah let out a whoosh of breath. In her favor? In her *favor*? That meant yes. Yes.

"As your grandmother and as the head of the Gallagher family, I was able to persuade the board to vote yes, despite your relationship with Mr. Trask. It's a solid plan, Dinah, and I appreciated the detailed and professional way you went about putting this together."

The board had voted yes and her grandmother was praising her. Had she fallen into an alternate universe?

"That being said, I think it's important we discuss the matter of Mr. Trask."

"The matter?"

"He's beneath you, Dinah. I hope you know that."

Dinah could only gape for a few buzzing seconds. "B-beneath me? That . . .that doesn't even make sense. What do you me—"

"You're a smart woman. You're strong and you're determined. You can make Gallagher's into something better than Craig can. I believe that. I'm willing to tell him, and the board, my opinion the next time the director position comes up for discussion and vote."

Dinah couldn't believe what she was hearing. Grandmother thought she'd do *better* than Craig. Dinah believed that wholeheartedly, but she hadn't considered Grandmother might agree with her.

"Grandmother. I don't . . . I don't know how to thank you. This is—"

"Thanks aren't necessary, because this is best. But, there is one condition."

All the elation, all the joy, all the pleased and touched parts of her came to a screeching halt. The glow of her grandmother's praise wore off pretty damn quick. "A . . . condition?"

"I will only support you as director under the condition that you are not romantically involved with Carter Trask."

It hit her like a blow. Hard and physical. She actually fell forward a little, as though someone had punched her straight in the back. She couldn't breathe, and when she managed to finally suck in a breath, she looked at her grandmother's shrewd hazel eyes and knew without a shadow of a doubt there was no arguing her way out of this.

This was Grandmother's ultimatum. Her final decision. The only hope of being the director of operations of Gallagher's, like she was supposed to be, was to lose Carter.

"I'm sure you think I'm being unfair, in the moment, but I saw the way that man stood up for you, and I see what you're doing for that man. Quite honestly, this isn't the lark Craig seems to think it is. You seem to care about each other."

"I do. We do. Grandmother—".

"Nevertheless, Carter Trask is not for you. If you're going to be the head of Gallagher's, if you're going to be our director of operations and take my place as matriarch of this family when I'm gone, you need someone who understands this world. Someone who knows when to shut his mouth. Someone who knows how to lie. For heaven's sake, that man did nothing but spout the truth in his proposal. It was god-awful."

"Grandmother," Dinah croaked.

"I suppose you think you love him or that he understands you or whatever young people think. I've been where you are, but this is the law of the Gallagher woman's life. The choice."

"I don't understand what I'm choosing," Dinah replied, feeling sick and teary and hoping to show neither of those things to her formidable grandmother.

"You're choosing Gallagher's. First and foremost. When you do that, you'll want a marriage that's more of a business proposition than love. I didn't marry your grandfather because he was the great love of my life. I married him because he would allow me to continue my work with Gallagher's. I married him because he was a businessman himself and understood. Love has no place in this family if you want to continue a legacy. Your uncle married for love. See what that got him?"

"Grandmother."

"Your young man is dedicated to his farm, and you found a way to combine farming with our business. Congratulations. Now, what happens at the first roadblock? The first time our business needs don't meet with his? What happens when we have to decide what is more important—Gallagher's bottom line or his?"

"It would be business. Something everyone worked through as business people. Just because Carter and I have a personal relationship doesn't mean it has to bleed into our professional one."

"You're young and idealistic. It doesn't work that way. The only way you can combine personal and professional is to do what I did. Trust me, Dinah. This is for your own good."

"You loved Grandpa," Dinah whispered, feeling small and young and stupid. This wasn't true, or right. It was just a test or something. "You did, and he loved you."

"We'd been married for over twenty-five years by the time you were born. We certainly grew to love each other in a fashion. We grew to love Gallagher's together. Will your man ever love Gallagher's more, or even as much, as he loves his farm?"

That landed like a blow too, because she knew the answer beyond a shadow of a doubt. Never. Carter would never love something more than his land. His roots.

"The reason Gallagher's is so important to us is because it's in our blood. It beats as our hearts. The person you end up marrying has to understand that at least half our hearts, if not all, is with Gallagher's. First and foremost. Before marriage. Before children. Before everything."

Dinah was shell-shocked and numb. She wasn't ready to think

about *marriage*. Love was still that scary thing she was trying to figure out, but giving it up before she figured it out seemed cruel.

"Those are my terms. You can take them or leave them."

"I don't know what to do." Dinah wasn't sure she'd ever admitted to her grandmother she didn't know something. That she was confused and hurt. A normal grandmother-granddaughter relationship would probably include something heartfelt or understanding, but Dinah was under no illusion that she'd get any of that.

"Take a few days to break it off with Trask, and when you do, come back to me. I'll make my recommendation to the board at that point."

Dinah blinked. This all felt surreal. Like it was happening to someone else. Like it wasn't real. "What about Craig? He won't take that well."

"You let me handle my son. I want your answer by Friday, Dinah."

She forced herself to stand and didn't even bother with a goodbye.

"I know you'll make me proud, Dinah," Grandmother said as Dinah walked out the door.

In her whole life all Dinah had wanted was to make her grandmother proud. Make Gallagher's proud. To take her *rightful* place.

Now here it was, within reach, and it was coming at such a cost. Dinah didn't know how to wrap her head around it, and she sure as hell didn't know what to do about it.

Carter was elbow deep in compost when Dinah finally showed up. He looked up at her. She was pale and drawn, and he immediately assumed the worst. "They voted no."

Dinah forced a smile and shook her head. "They voted yes. The partnership is a go."

"So why do you look like your dog just died?"

"Grandmother had *quite* a talk with me," she said, sounding small and far away, so unlike Dinah, he pushed to his feet.

"About?"

Dinah studied him long and hard. "You know, I don't really want to talk about it right now. It was all kind of personal stuff."

Carter rocked back on his heels. Personal. She said it in a way that seemed to insinuate he had nothing personal to do with her. *Ouch.*

"Did you want to celebrate? Because you seem kind of not in the mood for that."

"It's weird. I just don't know how to..." She swallowed and looked around his yard, so many emotions on her face he couldn't read them all. "Could you just kiss me?" She laughed, but there was no happiness behind it.

He reached out to touch her face, but he stopped because his hands were filthy. "Tell me what's wrong."

She looked away from him, and it was like the moment in the bar when her grandmother had dismissed him. She looked lost and confused, but he didn't know how to reach her.

"I just don't even know. Nothing today quite went the way I anticipated and...I...I think I need to go talk to Kayla. Kayla would know what to do."

"Okay. But, you know, you could talk to me too. I might have a few ideas."

She forced a smile that was probably the most fake thing he'd ever seen.

"It's just such crazy family stuff. I think I can explain it better if I talk to her first."

"Baby, I'm worried about you. Can't you tell me what happened? You look like you're about to cry."

That's exactly what she did. She started to cry. Carter didn't have the last fucking clue what to do with that, but even with all the dirt and crap on his hands, he pulled her against him.

She cried into his shoulder for he didn't know how long, but as she slowly got ahold of herself he didn't miss how tense she felt.

Eventually she stepped away, refusing to make eye contact. "Well, that's embarrassing."

"It shouldn't be. It's okay to cry."

She made a sound, something he couldn't figure out—a scoff, a laugh, another sob?

"I have to go," Dinah said, shaking her head and backing away.

"You can't leave without telling me what's wrong. Come inside, I'll—"

"No, I really have to go," she whispered, backing away, step by step, still not meeting his gaze.

"Dinah."

"I'm sorry," she whispered, shaking her head and turning to leave.

He wanted to say something. A lot of somethings. But he bit his tongue. Whatever she was dealing with, she didn't want him to have anything to do with it. He'd been there. He knew how that went. People kept secrets and did what they wanted without his input.

That was life. Might as well accept it.

His gaze raked the yard, looking for something to pound or destroy to get this impotent anger out of him. Instead it landed on a person stepping through the gate as Dinah scurried out.

"I'm in no mood for another fight, Jordan," Carter called out, because he was afraid if Jordan tried to pick another fight with him, Carter wouldn't be able to stop himself from pounding his friend.

Jordan put his hands up. "I actually came to apologize for how I acted the other day."

"What changed your tune?"

"Grandma threatened to beat me with a wooden spoon?" Jordan laughed and shook his head. "Seriously, man, I was . . . I was worried about Grandma. She's been forgetting things. She fell. It was easier to worry about, well, the house and dumb shit than it was to worry about her."

"Yeah, man, I get that."

"So I'm sorry I jumped down your throat. Grandma even thinks this is a good thing, so I gotta agree whether I want to or not."

"If nothing else, I'll get the inside scoop on Gallagher's."

Jordan snorted. "The only inside scoop you're getting is on Dinah Gallagher herself."

Carter stiffened. He knew his friend was trying to make a joke, but nothing with Dinah felt particularly joke-like right now. So he didn't say anything to that; he focused on his last-of-the-season corn.

"You really got a thing for her, huh?"

Carter eyed Jordan, who was standing there watching him carefully. "Hell. I think I'm in love with the damn woman," he muttered.

"No shit."

Carter shook his head. He had no idea why he'd said that aloud, to Jordan of all people. He wasn't an effusive guy. Didn't talk about his problems or his damn feelings.

But he didn't know what to *do* with them.

"I hate change," Jordan said with a weary sigh. "People getting older. New partnerships. New . . . feelings and crap. It's all a load of bullshit."

"I'm inclined to agree with you, but you know what my dad always used to say about bullshit?"

"Some country hillbilly saying that will make no damn sense to me?"

"Bullshit grows the best produce."

Jordan barked out a laugh. "I'd rather have a way to stop time than a damn big tomato."

"It ain't that magical."

Again Jordan laughed, and though Carter was still worried about Dinah, it felt good to laugh, to remember a thing his dad had said about hard times, and commiserate a bit on how good stuff can grow from difficult stuff.

He'd lost his land time and time again, but always found more land, and more meaning. He'd lost Grandma, and that would always hurt, but Dinah had been a salve for his grief. Company and care. Someone to lean on even if she didn't have a clue he was leaning.

"So, you going to go after her?" Jordan asked, nodding toward Gallagher's.

Carter assumed she'd gone to talk to Kayla, and maybe she needed that. To talk to family, people who understood all the weird Gallagher's dynamics. He'd give her that time, but then . . .

"Soon enough," he returned. "Soon enough."

# Chapter 16

Dinah was a mess, and she'd never been a mess before. Even after her family life had exploded into what it was now, she'd never fallen apart like this. She'd still had a plan and a goal and a focus.

Now she was confused and lost and, most problematic of all, needing someone else's advice. She couldn't ask Carter, not when this was about them, though she had the sneaking suspicion the man in her life she'd known the least amount of time might understand her the best.

Still, this wasn't as easy as understanding. This was choosing, and it was a choice she'd never imagined having to make. She'd been certain her whole life she could have it all—everything she wanted—if she only worked hard enough.

Was it all a lie?

She didn't particularly want to ask Kayla for advice when Kayla was having a break with Gallagher's and the family. But Kayla knew the family, knew Grandmother, knew *Dinah*. Surely she could put aside her feelings about Gallagher's in order to give advice.

Dinah thumped her head against Kayla's apartment door in lieu of knocking. She felt like she needed to knock her head against something hard about a hundred more times before today would make sense.

When Kayla opened the door, she was a little breathless and flushed, and her eyes widened as she took in Dinah. "You've been crying," she said by way of greeting.

"Hi to you too."

Kayla opened the door farther and ushered Dinah inside.

"Did that bastard hurt you?" Kayla demanded.

"Bastard? You mean Carter?"

Kayla nodded emphatically and Dinah smiled, because even with things not quite normal between them, Kayla was being protective.

"He's been great," Dinah assured her.

"Then why are you crying? You never cry. I assumed it had to be a guy."

"Not exactly yes and not exactly . . ." It was then Dinah realized there were boxes everywhere. Dinah could only blink and stare at the evidence Kayla was . . . getting ready to move? "What's going on?" Dinah demanded, pointing at a half-packed box.

"Let's focus on you right now."

"But you're moving!"

"Not far, and it's not important right now. What's far more important is that you're crying. What's wrong?"

"I take it you didn't hear your father's screech of rage from ten blocks away?"

Kayla frowned. "Dad hasn't spoken to me since I quit."

"Carter and Simone and I presented our idea to the board, and they approved it. We'll be working with Carter to create a completely local portion of the menu."

Kayla smiled. "That's great. Really. It's a fantastic idea, and I hope it works out. But that doesn't explain why you're upset."

"Grandmother summoned me into her office."

"Oh." Kayla let out a long breath and started moving boxes off the couch. "We need to sit for this."

"How do you know?"

Kayla gave Dinah a nudge onto the couch before taking a seat next to her. "Grandmother never brings us into her office unless it's bad. In fact, the only time she's ever had me come in her office was when I quit."

"How did that go? You haven't talked to me. I didn't . . ." Dinah hadn't tried, which wasn't like her either, but Kayla's rejection of Gallagher's felt like a personal rejection too.

Kayla looked away, but there was an odd smile on her face. "I needed a clean break from all things Gallagher, and I love you, Dinah, so much, but I knew you didn't understand that. But it was good. I mean, does it suck that Dad won't talk to me and Grandmother's cutting me off? Sure. But I needed it. I *need* it. So I'm fine. You're the one crying."

"I hate that we fought." Because she'd missed this. Missed her cousin and her friend.

"I do too, and I think I'm getting close to a place where . . . I just . . . I don't want anything to do with Gallagher's right now. Not Dad. Not Grandmother."

"Not me."

Kayla sighed. "I will gladly accept Dinah my friend and my cousin, but Dinah Gallagher, future director of operations, is not welcome in my life right now. I'm really sorry, but for once I have to do something that's right for me."

"But those things are all me! They interconnect and I can't keep them separate. I tried with Carter, and even that didn't work. I am Gallagher's in my bones. I can't be only your friend or only your cousin. I'm all of it."

"It sounds like you need a break," Kayla said gently.

"I do not need a break." Dinah jumped to her feet, panic giving her the energy she'd been missing. "I'm not taking a break. Gallagher's is everything to me."

Kayla looked away. "I love you, but maybe you should go."

Dinah felt the tears rushing back all over again, and she hated this. She hated being a whiny crybaby all of a sudden, but nothing was going right and everything felt hard.

"Before I go, will you just . . . let me just tell you this." Her voice was wavering and the tears were threatening, but she had to talk to someone.

She knew how Carter would feel about it. It would hurt his feelings and he would get weird, and she couldn't talk to him about it until she knew exactly what she wanted to do. Then she could convince him whatever she needed to do was the right thing. But she couldn't do that until she knew what was right.

Kayla waited, sad blue eyes downcast, and Dinah had to swallow the lump in her throat.

"Grandmother told me she would suggest me to the board as director of operations instead of Craig, on one condition."

Kayla's soft expression changed immediately. "Let me guess: The condition was totally realistic and normal and not at all insane."

"She said I can't be in a personal relationship with Carter. That he'd never be the type of husband I'd need—to be her."

"Do you really want to be *Grandmother?*" Kayla said it with such disgust, as if Grandmother wasn't everything Dinah had wanted to be and was afraid she couldn't live up to.

"Oh my God," Kayla breathed, her eyes going wide. "You *do* want to be her!"

"She's amazing. She's strong and everyone listens to her and . . . no one questions her." No one abandoned her or pushed her aside. She was *power*, and Dinah had always wanted that kind of . . . certainty of her place in the world.

"There are a lot of amazing things about Grandmother, I will give you that, but she's also incredibly cruel and unfeeling. Is that who you really want to be?"

"You say that like I have a choice."

"Of course you do! We have a choice. We've *always* had a choice, Dinah. You *choose* to think Gallagher's is your heart and soul."

"No, I don't. It's how I was born." She believed that. She *had* to believe that. If she thought she had a choice, if she deserted like Kayla and her father, what did that make her? She knew exactly what.

A failure. Alone. No one.

"Bullshit. It's easy, is what it is. It's safe. You know, I thought I was the coward in this relationship, but now I'm not so sure."

Dinah wanted to stand up for herself. She wanted to argue or say nasty things back, but it hurt so damn much, and she was already so raw. "Why are you being so mean to me lately?"

"Because I love you and I see this pattern in the things you do. Things get hard and you hyper-focus on the wrong thing. You're in such incredible denial about yourself and your worth, and I'm tired of pretending like I don't see it, to spare your feelings."

"Denial? My worth? Come on, Kayla, I—"

"You haven't dealt with anything that happened in the past year. Not your father, not how it affects you as a *person*, not just at Gallagher's. Things have changed. It's time you changed with them. If you want to be Grandmother, be Grandmother. Break up with Carter. Run Gallagher's. Turn into an old woman who everyone is afraid of, and no one *loves*."

"I'm going to go."

"Oh, no. I gave you a chance, but you asked. You will hear me out. You can choose to lose everything about you that makes me love you—your warmth and your honesty and your humor and your caring." Kayla stood up, standing in front of her, looking as fierce as Dinah had ever seen her.

"I never understood, Dinah, because you're not like them. You care so much about people—not just that goddamn waste of space. You care about the people who make up that business, and if you want to get to the point where you don't anymore, the point where all you see are dollar signs and reputation, and whatever it is they see, then go ahead. You can do all that, you can *choose* all that, but I don't think that's what you really want. If it was what you really wanted, you'd have already got after it. You'd have broken up with Carter without a second thought."

"It isn't that easy."

"No, it's life. It isn't easy, but it is something you have to do. Just like leaving is something I have to do. We're at the point where we have to choose for ourselves, but it is a choice."

"I'm in love with him," she said, wishing the words back the minute they escaped, raw and confused.

That stopped Kayla in her tracks though. "You're in love with . . . Carter Trask?"

"I don't want to be. I shouldn't be." She started pacing between Kayla's mountains of boxes. "But I can't seem to get rid of that feeling. I can't fight it. All of these feelings are there, and I am in love with him."

"Have you told him?"

Dinah shook her head. "No. I wasn't sure of it, and then Grandmother dropped this bomb, but love is just like the business thing. There has to be a compromise."

"Eventually people run out of compromises, Dinah. Trust me. I certainly ran out of mine. Tell him. Show him. Don't let Grandmother take this from you."

"If I choose him, I lose everything that was always supposed to be mine." She forced the words out past the fear, past maybe some of that denial Kayla was accusing her of having. But how could she lose what she'd always wanted, give it up for something that had come out of the blue? That could end, and hurt her?

"Yours? Maybe our lives aren't ending up like we planned, but maybe there is a new, different path we're supposed to take."

"I refuse to take any path that takes me away from Gallagher's," Dinah said harshly, feeling harsh but certain. She'd always been certain. This had always been her. How could that change? "Gallagher's is my heart and soul. I can't let that go."

"Then you need to leave," Kayla said, shaking her head. "Because you're not here to actually listen to what I have to say."

Dinah could see the tears in Kayla's eyes, hear the hurt in her voice. It matched Dinah's own. "I don't know when hating Gallagher's happened, or why it means you can't be my best friend anymore."

"I don't know either. But if you're willing to put a building over love, then I don't really want to be your friend."

"That's not what I'm doing," Dinah said, tears spilling over again, her heart cracking into pieces no matter how hard she tried to hold it together.

"Isn't it?"

Dinah had never been so confused or lost in her entire life. She never in her wildest dreams would have thought her friendship with Kayla would end, would change. But she didn't know how to bridge this gap.

"I guess I'll see you around then," Dinah muttered, heading for the door.

"Yeah," Kayla replied.

And that was it. Walking out of Kayla's apartment, it felt like . . . like a million things had felt in the past year, and she had to shove it down, shove it away, because if she let it, it would win. Demolish her.

It wasn't denial, it was survival.

Instead of heading for Carter and his Front Yard Farm, where she'd been spending all of her non-Gallagher's time lately, she headed home.

Like so many things in her life, no one could fix this for her, but she'd be damned if she wouldn't find a way to fix it herself. Kayla was wrong. She had to be.

Carter had never been one for poking his nose in other people's business, especially the business of women he was sleeping with. He'd typically had plenty of his own issues to focus on. Why take on someone else's?

Dinah was different, because of course she was. She had been *different* from the start.

That didn't mean he particularly liked sitting in front of her apartment door like some lovelorn idiot. Or that he had any damn clue what he'd say to her when she showed up.

"Suck it up, Trask," he muttered. He'd partnered with Gallagher's, of all damn places, because of Dinah. The least he could do was see the whole . . . relationship aspect through.

Something had happened with her grandmother today, and the supportive boyfriend type person needed to stand up and support and comfort.

Shit, what had he gotten himself into?

"Carter?"

He turned to Dinah, who was walking down the hallway to her apartment. "Hey."

"Hey." She paused before slowly taking steps toward him. "I . . ." She let out a breath and he thought she was maybe trying to smile, but it was mostly just a grimace.

"We don't have to talk about things," he said, hoping to put her somewhat at ease.

She blinked and looked down as she approached her door. "I'm not really up for sex either."

He squeezed his eyes shut, feeling like an idiot. "That's not what I meant. No. I just . . ." He watched as she unlocked her door, looking as fragile as he'd ever seen her. Maybe he hadn't known her for that long, but he knew this wasn't *like* her.

"I just wanted to be, like, supportive or whatever."

She pushed her door open and looked at him quizzically. "Supportive?"

"You're going through something, and you don't want to talk about it yet, but I didn't . . . You didn't say you wanted to be alone, so . . . Am I fucking this all up?"

"No." She stepped inside, then pulled him in behind her. "You're being very sweet after a day when people have been . . . not, and I don't know how to . . ." She shut the door behind him and flicked the deadbolt. Then she leaned against the door and took a deep, shuddery breath.

"I just wanted to . . . You know, when you care about someone you want to give them what they need when they're struggling."

"I don't know what I need."

"How about we start with this." He pulled her into his arms, gathering her close and hoping to offer some kind of comfort. Not words, not sex, just . . . that thing he and his sisters had done after Mom had died. You rallied around, you held on, you gave what you could and hoped it was some measure of comfort.

The way she relaxed into him, exhaling deeply, wrapping her arms around him and burrowing in, he liked to think he'd given her just that.

She nuzzled closer. "You care about me?" she asked, her voice muffled in his shoulder.

He ran his fingers through the strands of her hair, rubbing up and down her spine with his other hand. He liked this, probably more than he should. That she'd lean on him, that she'd ask for something from him. That she'd trust him enough for both.

"Yeah." He cared. Hell, he was probably in love with her, and now wouldn't be such a bad time to say it. Maybe. Or maybe it was the worst time and he was an idiot. "Dinah, I . . ."

"I care about you too, you know. I wouldn't be here . . . It wouldn't even be a question."

He pulled her away gently, wanting to see what was going on in her expression so he could maybe read this. "What wouldn't be a question?"

Her eyes widened and she looked a little panicked, and he wished she would be honest with him. Just open, so he could *get* it.

But maybe if he wanted her to be honest with him, it had to start with him. It wasn't honest to hold her and offer words of care without telling her the whole thing. The whole, big, scary-as-fuck thing.

"It's . . . it's more than care, Dinah."

She sucked in a breath and held it there. It was funny that *now* the panic left her expression, and she was only looking at him in a wide-eyed silence she didn't even breathe through.

Considering she just kept holding her breath, he figured he'd better force himself to say it. Just blurt it out and deal with the fallout, because he wasn't a coward. He faced his shit head-on. "I'm in love with you. Which I would not have believed possible in a million years that day you tried to pick my unripened squash."

She let out a breath, eyes still wide but watery now too. "That sounds *so* dirty," she whispered.

He laughed, though he didn't know how he managed it when his heart was pounding and his gut was twisting into a hundred tiny but heavy and painful knots. "I'd make an even dirtier squash joke, but I'm not sure I have it in me right now."

She stepped closer then, though they were already close. This was like a step into him, her palms resting on his shoulders, her breasts brushing his chest, her legs stepping into the sturdy shelter of his.

Her dark hazel eyes searched his face for something, though he didn't know what. There were so many things she was searching for, determined to find and achieve. It scared the daylights out of him that love might be the last thing she wanted, that it'd never be enough for her.

But she curled her fingers into his shirt, and she looked right at him. "I love you too, though I'll also have to agree on the not-having-a-clue part. It snuck up on me and grabbed ahold of me and I don't know how to shake it off."

He pressed his fingers into her shoulders, a reassuring squeeze. "I don't think you have to when we're in mutual agreement on the subject."

Her mouth curved, but Carter didn't think it constituted as a smile. She was probably scared, or maybe nervous. Maybe, like him, she'd never given so much to a relationship before. Even being quite certain of his feelings for her didn't make the feelings easy, or magically let him know what to do or say.

"What does it mean?" she asked, her hands curling into his shirt even tighter. "To all the other things in our life? All those other important things. I don't know how to make room for . . . love. Another person, other hopes or dreams. I've only ever had my own."

"I don't know either. I've never made room before." Hell, he wasn't sure he'd ever been this honest before. Not so plainly and with someone he wasn't related to, that was for sure. "I don't think it's easy, but I think you're just supposed to keep working at it until it fits or gels or something."

She chewed on her lip for a few seconds, and he had to admit this wasn't exactly how he'd pictured a declaration of love. He'd assumed confessions of that nature usually got sealed with a kiss, sex, anything but staring at each other, floundering already.

"I need you to do me the biggest favor," Dinah said, though her voice was barely louder than a whisper. But she was earnest, fierce. "I need you to hear me out, listen to my *whole* story without . . . walking away."

"That sounds bad."

"It isn't good, but we can figure it out." He recognized the look on her face, the determined glint in her eye. Recognized the way she made a decision and then held on to it with everything she had in her.

He loved that about her, that fierceness and dedication and certainty, but it also concerned him, because he wasn't always so sure that fierceness *was* certainty. Sometimes it seemed she went after things simply because she had it in her head that it was the only way—not because it was *actually* the only way.

"We've figured it out so far," she continued. "You said it yourself, you keep working at it until it fits or gels or something."

But Carter knew what it looked like when love came with impossible strings and impossible dilemmas, and shouldn't he have known better with a Gallagher?

But she'd said *I love you*. They'd said it to each other. Surely this thing couldn't be so bad.

"My grandmother gave me an ultimatum."

Or maybe it could.

# Chapter 17

Dinah had an idea. It had popped into her head sometime between his saying he cared about her and he loved her.

*Loved.*

She didn't want to give this up. She didn't want to sacrifice one dream for another, so she wouldn't. Compromise. All it would take was a little bit of compromise, and phrasing this the exact right way.

"What kind of ultimatum, Dinah?"

"Let's sit down. Do you want something to drink? I could—"

"Dinah."

He wasn't giving her any time at all to think, to plan, to prepare, but she couldn't exactly leave him hanging either.

He loved her. *Love.* He'd offered her a hug and wanted to comfort and support her without even knowing what was going on. She owed him something, and she could think quickly on her feet.

She met his worried gaze, and it wasn't hard to see the toll his heart had taken in a lifetime. Losing pieces of himself and fighting his family to keep them, he was braced for the worst.

She wouldn't let this be the worst. "My grandmother doesn't approve of you."

"My shock, it is huge," he intoned, sarcasm dripping from every syllable.

"She said if I would cut personal ties with you, she would recommend me for the director of operations position over Craig."

Finally, he sat, reminding her of a big tree falling over after having been cut. Her couch even let out an audible groan at the sudden influx of weight.

"Well, you could have mentioned that before we started talking about love."

"No, because they are two separate things," she said firmly. Two different wells of love, and she would find a way to drink from them both, damn it.

He shook his head. "Dinah, come on. They are not two *separate* things. Not in your world."

"We found a way to get around the whole buy-your-land thing. This will be easy compared to that."

"No, it won't. This is pretty clear. To get what you've always wanted, you've got to kick me to the curb."

He seemed so certain, but he didn't understand. If only he'd given her more time, she would have had the perfect spiel to convince him. She couldn't give up, though. She had to keep trying to get him to understand. "You're what I've always wanted too."

He sighed, raking his hands through his shaggy hair. "That doesn't make sense."

"Yes, it does. Despite everything that's happened, I *know* there was a time when I was growing up that my parents loved each other. I saw my grandparents love each other." No matter what Grand-mother said. "I have seen love in action and I've always wanted that. I don't believe I have to sacrifice one dream for another. I refuse to let that be true."

He looked at her, not as though he believed her, or even as though he wanted to, but with a pained kind of expression in his dark eyes. "I know that you . . . God knows you can make miracles happen, but I don't think this is one of them."

"But I do. I believe that this is definitely one of them and I can accomplish exactly what I want to. You know why I keep being able to do that?"

"Luck?"

"Determination," she returned firmly. "Because I don't give up. Because I believe. All it takes is that belief, and hard work, and no matter what the setback, you can get where you want to be. I believe that. I have to believe that."

"I don't know how to believe that, Dinah. I have done those things, I have believed and worked my ass off and hoped so hard, but I have lost. Repeatedly."

"Then you fell in love with the right person. I will believe enough for the both of us." She knew he didn't see it. He didn't believe it. She could even understand that. He'd had a lot of crap happen to him and it hadn't worked out.

But she had to believe that meant he hadn't tried hard enough. He had given up too soon. She was going to make this work because she wouldn't give up. Period. Nothing could stand in her way.

"How exactly are you proposing to get the director job and have a relationship with me when your grandmother gave you such a clear ultimatum?"

That was the tricky part, and she hadn't quite worked out everything. With more time to think and plan she could make it sound better. She worried her hands together, trying to find the right words. The not-insulting words.

"You don't have a plan, do you?" he said, his voice so quiet and so final. How could he be so easily discouraged?

"Yes, I do. I'm just working out how to explain it."

He narrowed his eyes at her suspiciously, and she almost couldn't blame him for that. It didn't exactly sound good. Maybe she should just say it instead of trying to find the perfect combination of words. "I guess the bottom line is that there's no reason Grandmother has to know we're together."

"How is that a plan?"

"All we have to do is hide our relationship for little while. It doesn't mean we actually have to be apart. She just has to think we are."

"Your uncle followed you. I actually think we would very much have to be apart to convince anyone of our being apart."

"But once I replace Craig, it won't matter. They won't re-replace me with him."

"Why not?"

Frustration was starting to mount. It seemed he had a question for everything. Couldn't he trust her? Couldn't he *believe*? "Because they will see what an excellent job I'm doing and how much better I am than he was."

"That is so incredibly optimistic."

"You don't understand the family dynamics here, and you don't understand how important Gallagher's is. Once they see what I can do in that position, they won't want anyone else in it."

"So, just to get this all straight, your plan as to how to get both things you want is to pretend like you don't have one of them. And I'm supposed to go along with being your dirty little secret?"

She frowned. She wasn't sure she'd ever get used to how easy it was for him to hurt her. She usually had a thick skin, but something about him, or love, made everything seem pointed. Harsh. "It's not like that."

Still, she couldn't give in to that hurt, because that would be admitting some kind of defeat, and she refused. She kneeled in front of him, because he had to see. "It's not about being a dirty little secret. It's not about being ashamed. It's just working around them because they're wrong. Grandmother is wrong."

He rubbed a hand over his face before looking down at her, and she knew that even though he wasn't falling into line quite as she'd like, he was feeling all this too. It wasn't easy for him.

"Is she?"

Another few words that seemed to lance hard and sharp, right where it would hurt most. "How can you tell me you love me and ask me that at the same time?"

He shook his head and looked away, and panic bubbled up, but she wasn't going to let panic win. She was right. All of the things she'd accomplished were because she was *right*, because she had believed without a shadow of a doubt she was the correct party. If it had worked her whole life so far, how could she stop believing that if she felt it was right, she just had to keep pushing?

"I know my grandmother seems like this crazy and perhaps formidable person. But she's just . . . wrong. She doesn't understand everything. You don't understand Gallagher's itself, but you understand me. And how much it means. I wouldn't be talking about compromise if you didn't mean so much."

"I know. I'd go so far as to say your dedication to that place is one of the things I love about you. But, Dinah, if everyone there is going keep putting us at odds, I don't know how we keep doing this. Eventually you're going to have to choose. One or the other."

He was so earnest, so sure in his defeat, but she refused to be. She refused to acknowledge defeat. "No, I do not. I'll keep finding compromises and ways around it. I know I will."

"I appreciate your optimism, I do, but I don't know that I can match it. I don't know that I can be . . . You're asking me to believe our relationship is something you're never going to walk away from.

But I know the thing you're never going to walk away from is Gallagher's, and I wouldn't *want* you to. But, eventually, you'll come to that point. That's how life works. You'll have to choose between this life you always planned and this," he said, gesturing to the distance between them.

He was so earnest, and she knew he was being honest and open, but he was *wrong*. Why couldn't he see he was wrong?

"I've been where you are, Dinah. Maybe not with a romantic relationship, but I know what it's like to go up against people you love and work with. You want to believe you can handle whatever comes, and I want to believe too, but I've been down the road too many times to actually think . . ."

She rested her hand on his knee and squeezed, hoping some physical contact would get through to him. "I will be in charge once this all goes through, and then I can do whatever I want."

"You really think so?"

"Why are you being such a pessimist?" she demanded in frustration, letting her hand slide off his knee. She needed to ball it into a fist to try to keep her irritation at bay.

"Because that is who I am." He reached out and touched her face and she leaned into that rough, gentle touch.

"I'm not giving up on this." She couldn't. It was . . . so wonderful to be in love. It was scary, but exhilarating. Hard, but just . . . the moments like this, leaning into him, talking, it was more than she'd imagined that love would be. It was big. It was a challenge, but damn, she was good with a challenge.

"I'm not saying I'm giving up either," he said, rubbing his thumb back and forth across her cheek as he cupped her jaw. "I'm just saying if you ignore all of the complexity and challenges that are going to be put before you, it will not go well."

"It's not complex. All we have to do is have a secret relationship for a while. It won't be all that different from when we were emailing and it was a secret even to us." She grinned at him, but there was no humor in him, no lightening.

"Here's the thing." He looked her straight in the eye, the light graze of his fingers never wavering, and it made her heart flutter and dive, even though she knew—damn it all, she knew—it wasn't going to be a good *thing.*

"I don't want to go back to that," he said, firm and sure. "If I wasn't in love with you, maybe it would be fine to be a secret, or to pretend, but that's not what I want this to be. It's not what it should be." He dropped his hand and stood, pacing away from her.

For the first time her heart fluttered in fear. She'd been so certain he would agree, but this seemed very close to him refusing. Flat-out.

"It'd just be for a little while," she said, embarrassed at how *weak* and *pleading* she sounded.

"You say that, but if your grandmother doesn't approve now, she's never going to approve. That's fine. I don't need your grandmother's approval any more than I need my own family's approval, but I think you do."

She got to her feet. "I do not."

"If you didn't, Gallagher's wouldn't be the thing you've been working for, your whole life. If your family didn't matter, if their feelings didn't matter, it wouldn't be your roots. There has to be some love of family and wanting to please them, to be as completely consumed by it as you are."

"I love Gallagher's because it is my soul." She fisted a hand to her heart. "Because I was born that way. Because it grew into my blood and into my bones. Gallagher's is me, and how I handle that, how I involve myself in it, has nothing to do with making my family happy."

"You were willing to buy my land even though you didn't agree with your uncle about its use."

"I was doing what I had to do to get what belongs to me," she returned through gritted teeth. "What I always planned." Why was he being so damn difficult about this?

"Good for you. Good for you for getting what you always planned, but it doesn't always work that way for all of us. Some of us never get what we planned."

"Is that what this is about? You're jealous."

She didn't know how they'd turned this into a fight. She didn't know why he was questioning her like Kayla had questioned her. Why he, of all people, couldn't understand this was what she needed.

"You know what? Maybe I am. Because you have everything I didn't get. Now you want me to believe in something while ignoring everything I know. From my experience. From my life. You're not listening to me at all. You're just marching on this path you have in your own brain and you won't . . . Why should I stand here and compromise with you when you won't compromise with me?"

"I am compromising. If I wasn't compromising, you wouldn't *be* here. I would've broken it off with you. I love you and I want to make this work, so here I am. Fighting." *Because I have an ounce of courage, asshole*, she barely restrained herself from saying.

"Okay. Let's say we do this. It's a secret, you get your director position, and no one catches us. What about the next thing?"

She blew out an annoyed breath, fisting her hands on her hips. "What do you mean, the next thing?"

"In the few short weeks we've been together, we've run into two huge challenges that require you to choose between Gallagher's and us. So, what about the next time? The time after that? What about the time when there is no choice, and there is no compromise? Who do you choose?"

"Both. I will find a way to have both." How could he not see that she wasn't going to lose this fight? She didn't lose, not Dinah Gallagher. *Gallaghers don't fail.* Grandmother's words, which would prove to be the thing Dinah needed to win.

"Dinah . . ." He linked his fingers behind his head, looking at her with such pain in his eyes she almost forgot about her frustration with him. "I don't know that I can put my heart on the line for another damn thing I know I'm going to lose."

"What do you want me to say to that? That I would pick you? That I would give up everything I love and I've built, for you?" How could he ask that of her, when she was saying they could have both?

"I don't want to ask that. I don't. I don't want you to choose me over Gallagher's. I'd never in a million years want that for you."

"But?" she demanded, because there was a *but*, and how dare he? How dare he care and love and be sweet, but not be willing to bend a little?

"But maybe this is impossible. Maybe there is no compromise. No answer. Because no matter how much we love each other, I don't know that either of us would ever pick each other over the things we've built."

"We won't have to make that choice. I believe in us, in what we can do, if we try hard enough."

"I don't believe in that, Dinah. I can't."

It was Dinah's turn to sink into the couch like a tree falling in the forest, because no matter how much she believed, if he didn't, she didn't know how to make this work.

Carter felt hollowed out. He'd finally fallen in love with someone, admitted it, and stood there ready to take that leap, and it had spiraled into this other place. A place he recognized all too well.

He wanted to be as certain as she was. He wanted to believe as firmly as she did, but that belief had been beaten out of him, and he didn't want to do it anymore. He didn't want to put his heart on the line when there was no chance he was going to keep the thing he was risking it all for.

"I don't know what you want me to say to that," Dinah finally said, clearly hurt that he didn't believe the way she did.

"I don't want you to say anything. I just think we need to go into this with our eyes wide open."

"And you refuse to believe?"

"I don't know *how* to believe anymore." Which was something maybe he'd known about himself but had tried to ignore, to push away. Leave it to Dinah to make him face it head-on, to make him say it out loud, to face the things he didn't want to face.

She stood and grabbed his arms, her eyes too warm, too sure. He wished he could believe, for her. That he could get over all of these hurts and cuts and wounds that had never healed.

"If you just believed in *me*. If you just . . . I can do it. I know I can. All you have to believe is that I know what I'm doing and I can make this work."

He didn't know how to do it. Not for her. Not for him. Her hands dropped off his arms and she stepped away.

"But you won't." She swallowed, and when she spoke again, her voice was broken. "You refuse to."

"I guess I do." He shook his head, because how had this all gone so completely off the rails? But he didn't know how to give her what she wanted. He didn't know how to believe anymore, and he didn't know how to give over all those feelings to her when he knew she would pick Gallagher's over him. There was no question in his mind, and that was fine. He understood it. Would he choose her over his farm?

That he even paused, even questioned it for a second, was enough to know that love or not, this wasn't what either of them needed. How could he ever question keeping the farm above all else?

Some weird bubble of panic squeezed his lungs, and he couldn't do this. Couldn't think these things, wonder these things. Couldn't question himself like this, and mostly he just couldn't believe. Wouldn't, like she said. "I should go."

"I guess you should," she returned, her voice vibrating with all kinds of hurt as she raised her chin at him. "You might want to look up the definition of love when you get home, because this isn't it. Maybe you like me and the sex is great, but I don't think this is love."

It shouldn't make him angry. It did, but he knew it *shouldn't*, so he fought to maintain a calm demeanor. "Maybe I don't have enough in me anymore." It thrummed through him, that lie. He *loved* her, too damn much. Why couldn't she see it wasn't enough? "Some of us continually get beaten down by life, while the rest of us get everything we want." Which was a damn petty thing to say, but he was struggling to care, even with the roil of guilt in his gut.

"Mature, Carter. Blame me. I've gotten everything easy. You've gotten nothing, even though you've worked hard. But I don't feel bad for you. I don't feel sorry for you. You have persevered and built things. You're fine. Maybe a whiny ass, but fine."

"Now who's being mature?"

She pointed to her door, shaking with anger, not that he could blame her. He was damn angry too. Furious, at himself, at her, at the damn world.

"Get out of my apartment," she demanded.

"Gladly." He walked out full of regret and shame, but mostly what made his throat tight and his chest constrict was more than shame or fear or hurt. It was more than not knowing how to believe and how to help.

It was understanding that no matter how he tried or moved or worked, loss was always around the corner. He thought he had built something, and it was swept away.

It didn't seem to matter whether he believed or not, whether he worked hard or not. Mom and Grandma had died. His dad had sold and left, his sisters had left.

For the first time in a long time, he'd felt hope and love again, thinking his relationship with Dinah could be different. But it wasn't.

He didn't know who to blame. He didn't know how to accept it. It wasn't selling off land, or death. It wasn't an irrevocable thing, out of his control.

This was something far more complicated, and possibly his own damn fault.

# Chapter 18

Dinah didn't sleep. She tossed and she turned and she cried, but she most definitely didn't sleep.

When 4:00 a.m. rolled around, she figured it was a lost cause. She might as well get up and go to work.

She hated Carter for making things so confusing. For taking all her certainty and mixing it with insecurity. She was sure she loved him. She was sure they could work it out, but not if he didn't want to.

She didn't regret the words she'd said to him. She didn't have any sympathy for him when he had worked so hard and overcome so much. How could he not know how strong and invincible that made him?

How could he not know that when he lost things, he just built something new and worked even harder? She admired that about him so much. She didn't know how to tell him that she had to believe, and she had to fight, and she had to be certain in order to do it all. She didn't know if she could rebuild like he had. She knew Carter could stand up and fight and start over and she . . .

She was so afraid of her inability to do that.

She got ready for the day feeling sick to her stomach and . . . just sad. Sad because he wasn't going to be showing up at her apartment offering her comfort. Sad because she didn't know what she felt or what to do. Every time in the past few weeks that she'd gotten a handle on things, life swept it all away. Kicked it out from under her. She couldn't get her footing. She'd move up the hill and then get knocked back.

It wasn't fair and she didn't like it.

In the dark of a fall morning, she drove to Gallagher's. She parked in the back, but instead of using the employee entrance, she walked around to the front.

She stood on the sidewalk, looking up at the place that had been her home and her life for as long as she could remember. It was . . . just a place. But it was hers. It was in her heart and her bones. She knew that.

But what did it give her?

Lately all it seemed to do was cause her to lose the people she cared about.

She tried to shake away the thought as the sun began to rise over the beautiful brick building that had stood there for a century. No matter how much she loved it, and she did with all of her heart and soul, it was just a building. It wasn't a friend to commiserate with. It wasn't a cousin to cry with over family drama. It certainly couldn't offer a hug when she felt like her world was falling apart. It couldn't say *I love you.*

She didn't know how to give it up, but she didn't know how to sacrifice those other things for it either. For the first time in her life, Dinah didn't know what to do or what to feel when it came to Gallagher's.

"You're certainly here early."

Dinah jumped and screeched, then turned to face her grandmother, who was standing there on the sidewalk, leaning on the cane she rarely let anyone see.

"So are you," Dinah returned, shaky from surprise and nerves.

"I like to watch the sunrise over what I've built." Grandmother smiled an odd smile Dinah couldn't read, and took a seat on a little bench where people sat when there was a wait line.

"I see you're doing the same," Grandmother said, placing the cane to the side Dinah wasn't standing on.

"I suppose I am." Dinah returned her gaze to the building and the pearly pink sky. "Beautiful."

"It is. My father used to do this too. He would come read his morning paper right on this bench. It's one of the things about Gallagher's that I love so much. I can sit where my father sat and do what my father did. I can feel his presence."

"What about your own mark?"

Grandmother shook her head. "I've done a lot for Gallagher's over the years, and certainly I'm proud of my contributions. But the reason I come here even now is for the memories of the people I love."

"How surprisingly sentimental of you."

"Now, don't be cross. I am sentimental. About this place, about our legacy. The only love that matters is the love of your family. The rest can be sucked away, as you should know by your father's actions."

"But he's my family, and I can't trust that anymore, can I?" There was a pain there, a swirling, dark one she'd been trying to avoid for a year: Betrayal was one of those injuries that didn't get to heal, that her determination couldn't bulldoze over.

It swamped her, in the shadow of Gallagher's, in the shadow of her grandmother's words.

"I coddled him too much," Grandmother said with such certainty. As though that was all it could be. She'd coddled him. He'd turned into an adulterous asshole. "Both of them. I let them think they were kings of the world. Biggest mistake I ever made. I won't make the same mistake with you. Dinah, you could be everything I was, and more. Women in your generation have more respect, more opportunities. You could make this place something bigger than it is. I never thought it would be possible with my sons, but it's possible with you."

"What is it about me that gives you that confidence?" Maybe if she knew, it would fix all this pain and all this uncertainty, and all this *longing* for people who looked at Gallagher's like a curse or a poison.

"Because you've been willing to sacrifice anything and everything for Gallagher's. Nothing has ever gotten in your way. Your focus is laserlike. You're not wrapped up in ego like your uncle. You're not selfish like your father. You always wanted this role, and you know how important it is."

Her grandmother gave her so few positive words, Dinah couldn't help but be flattered, knocked flat. Grandmother was sitting there telling her she could be what she'd always wanted to be.

*But at what cost?* A year ago, the cost would have been nothing, and Dinah would have done everything in her power to grab it, to live up to Grandmother's words.

But something rang flat today, some cold fissure of fear undercut the pleasure of Grandmother's praise.

"If I'm that important to Gallagher's, why are you trying to manipulate my life?"

"Because I've been where you are, had to make the decisions you have to make, and I know how to make it work. I'm taking an active role, because my inactive role with my sons was not sufficient."

"You said you and Grandpa grew to love each other." Dinah didn't know why she kept circling back to that, but she'd seen their love. Recognized it.

"That happens when you marry someone. You live with them for years and have their children. Love can be grown, Dinah. It doesn't have to exist from the second you meet someone."

Dinah let that sit. The thing was . . . love had grown between her and Carter from that first email to their first meeting and everything in between. It felt fast, but it had been a surprisingly slow and careful process.

One that had given her what Gallagher's and her family never had: comfort and care. Someone who concerned himself with what she was feeling—not just what was best for Gallagher's.

It was weird to think about having kids in this moment, but she did want kids in the future. She wanted them to feel the same connection to Gallagher's that she did, but now she wasn't so sure she wanted to force these kinds of expectations on her future children. She wasn't sure she wanted to fall in love with someone *after* she'd had his children.

She just wasn't sure about anything. She sat next to her grandmother and took a deep breath. "Are you happy, Grandmother? Is this what you dreamed of when you married someone you didn't love and had kids and worked relentlessly for Gallagher's? Is this what you pictured and wanted?"

"Oh, Dinah, life is never what we picture or imagine. Even when it is."

Those words hit. Hard. So much like what Kayla and Carter had been saying to her lately. That plans don't always work out, and maybe they shouldn't.

She would never walk away from Gallagher's. It *was* her soul, but did that mean things needed to go exactly according to plan? Did she really have to be director of operations to be happy here?

Her hands shook, her eyes pricking with tears at the thought, but there was a kind of *lightness* with this question. A heavy weight lifted.

She glanced at her grandmother, who was watching Gallagher's with a certain reverence Dinah understood. She felt it too.

But it hit her with a certain clarity that she didn't want to be in her eighties looking at a building like it was her child. She wanted to be looking at her children and her grandchildren, feeling like she'd done right by them, like she'd done right by herself.

She wanted relationships that fulfilled her heart, *and* this place that was her soul. But not one at the cost of the other.

"I'm going to keep seeing Carter. I'm in love with him, and if that means I don't get the director of operations job, that's fine. I'll stay on in whatever role you and Craig allow me." In the silent aftermath of that blurting of information, an odd noise came out of her. Fear shot through her, but she didn't open her mouth to retract her words.

She didn't want to.

"And if I threatened to fire you if you continue to see him?"

Dinah hadn't seen that threat coming, though she probably should have. But the answer was simple. It was always her answer. "I'll fight you. I'll take it to the board. To anyone who'll listen. This is my rightful place. If my choice of romantic partner is your only reason for keeping me away from here, then I will do everything in my power to fight you, because that is wrong. I know it's wrong." A belief. A certainty. No one could take those things away from her.

She was sure. She just had to have some *flexible* surety. She had to step away from the life she'd always planned, and work on the life she *wanted*.

"You'll lose, Dinah."

"I won't stop fighting, Grandmother. And you can't live forever."

Grandmother eyed her and Dinah couldn't read her expression, but she didn't back down. She would fight for Gallagher's. And she would fight for Carter. They couldn't make her choose, because she would never give up on Gallagher's even if they fired her. She would never give up on Carter even if he hated her.

Because she loved them both, and even if it took her whole damn life, she wouldn't give them up.

Carter had a lot of regrets in his life. Mostly ones that he hadn't really been able to control or do anything about. There was a weird kind of freedom in those regrets. He hadn't been able to do anything about them. They were what they were, and that was life.

His regrets about Dinah were far different, and he couldn't brush them aside as though there was nothing he could do. There was no doubt in his mind he was at least a little bit to blame in this whole situation.

Maybe if he'd needed less from her, or healed that hurt he'd lived so many times, he would've been able to do the things she asked. He could've had a secret relationship, he could have believed, he could love, even knowing he'd never be the one she chose.

But what would it hurt him to pretend? What would it hurt him to have a secret relationship with her? All it would hurt was his pride and, well, maybe a little bit more than that. But was pride so important? He could have her if he wanted her.

Somehow he couldn't get over the feeling that it would all be pointless someday. Because he knew choices came whether you wanted them to or not, and ultimatums were made, and life didn't always make compromise possible. Sometimes life kicked you in the balls and made you take the hard way out.

He didn't want to be the carnage in her hard way out someday. Maybe it wasn't fair, but he couldn't get over what he felt. As much as he loved her, he understood the love she had for Gallagher's. It would always be a threat to their relationship.

He tried to think of it in terms of the farm. Maybe someday he'd have to choose between her and the farm. He wouldn't be able to choose her, but something in his heart was pierced at the thought. It scared him that he could think that maybe he *could* put her above the rest.

He'd left so many pieces of land and pieces of his heart behind, what would be one more, if it meant he could be with her?

He scrubbed his hands through his hair even though they were filthy with compost and dirt. But that thought kept *taunting* him— that he would give up this for her, even though it was the last piece of himself.

But was it? He would always have the years he put into this land. He would always know he'd built this, just as his childhood memories of the farm were always there. His.

Nothing lasted. Nothing stayed forever. Life always went on. If he could have his grandmother back, his mother back, his family here, would he be willing to give this up?

It wasn't even a question. To have those people he loved back in his life, he would give up anything. He loved Dinah, and even though he hated to admit it, and wished he could be different, he would give up his farm for her.

So, accepting a secret relationship, or accepting that Dinah didn't love him enough to make the same choice—that would always be too much to bear.

Carter sat back on his heels on the pathway and looked out at all that he had built in the past few years. It filled him with pride and filled him with a sense of accomplishment, but, God, he wanted Dinah here to feel that with him.

Against his will, his gaze drifted to Gallagher's. It was early. Dinah probably wouldn't be at work yet, but he could picture her there. In her ridiculous heels and put-together outfits and colorful makeup and the perfectly wavy hair. She made such a picture.

He didn't know how to live with her knowing he could always be sacrificed for Gallagher's, and he sure as hell didn't know how to live without her.

Which didn't make any damn sense considering he'd lived most of his life without her. But she'd walked in and given him something he'd lost along with all of the other losses in his life. Someone to hold him when the world sucked. Someone who made him laugh. Someone who sat on this porch with him and looked out at all he'd built with the same sense of satisfaction.

Maybe there was someone else out there like her. Someone else who could fill that spot. It was possible, but with the heavy outline of Gallagher's in the distance, he wasn't sure he'd ever be able to fully enjoy life with anyone other than Dinah.

He looked away from Gallagher's and back at his plants. Regardless of the riot of screwed-up feelings, he still had a farm to tend. Simone had emailed him some of her winter menu ideas, and he had to determine if he could supply her with the necessary produce.

He had half a fleeting thought to give up his partnership with Gallagher's, if only so he didn't have to see Dinah, but not only was that cowardly, he would lose something he wanted.

He wasn't sure he could accept never seeing Dinah again anyway. If they couldn't work it out, then at least he could see her doing the thing she loved so much.

"You need a radio out here or something."

Carter didn't whirl around, mostly because he thought he might be hallucinating.

"Radio, huh?"

"It would break up some of the silence, and then people couldn't hear you muttering curse words all the way out on the sidewalk."

Carter listened to the unmistakable sound of high heels clicking against the stone path as she moved closer.

Bracing himself, he slowly got to his feet and turned. Dinah looked as she always looked. Perfectly put together. Beautiful. Sexy as hell.

"I'm not really in the mood to fight," he said, keeping his hands at his sides by sheer force of will. What he really wanted to do was reach out, touch her, make her promises he couldn't keep.

"Good. Neither am I."

"I don't think there's anything we can talk about that we won't fight about."

"Per usual, you're wrong."

"Dinah." How the hell she made him want to yell and laugh at the same time was beyond him.

She linked her hands in front of her, and after weeks of paying attention, he'd finally realized that was her show of nerves. He softened, against his will.

"I talked to my grandmother this morning. I sat there and watched the sunrise over Gallagher's and I asked her if she was happy. If she was fulfilled."

Carter took a deep breath. Though the little sparkle of hope was starting in his chest, he tried not to believe it. She was probably here to try to convince him they should have a secret relationship, and that everything would be fine. She never let anything go, so why would he believe things had changed? She'd come here to badger him until he gave in.

Well, she was damn well going to be disappointed.

"She talked about Gallagher's and how proud she was that she'd built it. She talked about being disappointed in her children, and how I had all the markings of someone who could take over and make Gallagher's something great."

"She's no doubt right on the money. You can go now."

"I told her to shove it."

Carter barked out a surprised laugh. Leave it to Dinah to surprise him even now. "You did not tell your grandmother to shove it."

She smiled. He didn't want to be charmed and tricked into smiling right back, but he could hardly help it.

"Okay, I didn't tell her to shove it. But I did tell her I wouldn't stop seeing you."

"I think last night was a pretty good indicator—"

"That we love each other. And I do love Gallagher's and it matters to me a lot. I'll never want to cut ties with it, but between you and Kayla stepping away from me because of it, I realized it doesn't matter as much as people. It matters. It matters a lot, but it's not you and it's not Kayla. It's not friendship and it's not love. I don't want to be eighty-something and not feel satisfied about the relationships I have. Buildings can't love you back, and the business can't give you a heart."

Carter felt frozen. He couldn't breathe. She was saying all the right things. Exactly what he needed to hear, and he was afraid to trust it. Maybe it was a hallucination.

Dinah blew out a long breath and then stepped closer. Everything about her was dead serious. She wasn't manically trying to bulldoze him. She wasn't gripping onto this one idea, certain it would work.

She was calm and earnest. She was hopeful, but it wasn't the same as sure.

"Loving you is more important to me than being director of operations. I don't think I have to walk away from Gallagher's, but I do have to change my plans. Which, as you may have guessed, isn't easy for me to do. My whole life I have followed this one dream, this one goal, and it's . . . it's hard to let go."

"You don't have to." He didn't want her to. He didn't want to be the thing—

"I do. I do because I realized I want you more than I want it. I want Gallagher's, but I'm not going to be my grandmother. I don't want to be Uncle Craig or my father. I don't want to get to a certain place in my life and realize that because I followed this one thing, I screwed up everything else. I'd rather have everything else and realize I screwed up Gallagher's."

She still stood inches away from him, looking so imploring and beautiful. He wanted to cross the distance and fall at her feet, but . . . How could he be sure? How could he give in to this?

*How can you not?*

"That's a pretty big decision. Are you sure?"

"Positive, actually. I've done the screw-up-everything-else part already. Nothing Gallagher's can give me takes away that hurt or that pain, but when Gallagher's was making me feel like crap, you and Kayla both gave me something that made me feel better. I choose what makes me feel better. I choose the people who give me love. I love you and I want you over anything else. I know if we're together we can find a way to do the things we both love. Maybe not the way we planned, but some way."

Carter didn't know what to do with his hands, and he certainly didn't know what to say. He was half convinced he was dreaming. "Are you sure?" he repeated.

"What would I have to do to prove it to you?"

"I don't know. I don't . . . I'm not sure I know what to do with something good happening or someone choosing me."

"Well, you're going to have to figure it out," she said, stepping toward him. She placed her palm on his chest and it was only then he saw she was shaking a little bit. It was only then he realized she must be worried. But she met his gaze with a certainty and serenity he recognized; with that strength of purpose she always seemed to have, which he admired so much he wanted to emulate it.

"Because I choose you, Carter. I choose love, and you know when I make a choice I don't waver. So I need you to do the same."

He covered her hand with his and wrapped his fingers around it. Warm and strong, a force to be reckoned with that was for sure, and everything he wanted. Even if it hurt, having it was like . . . breathing. Necessary. "I love you, Dinah."

"I love you too."

He knew he had to say more. Words were important and powerful and she deserved them. But it was hard to well up the courage to look at her and let out the feelings that had always brought him loss.

Maybe more than that, he was afraid of the power the words would give her, when she already seemed to have so much over him, but he also knew how important this moment was. It would be part of the foundation they built the rest of their lives on. So he said what he was most scared to say.

"I was just working this morning and coming to the conclusion that I would give all this up for you if I had to. That as much as I love it, and as much as it's a part of me, I'd rather have the *people* I love than the *things* I love. If I had to choose, I would always choose you."

A tear dropped onto her cheek and she brushed it away with her free hand. "I choose you, too. I do."

Carter had learned not to be certain. He'd learned to work with his head down, without hoping for the best or knowing that the best was around the corner. He'd learned not to think about the future and just focus on his present.

But with Dinah in front of him, choosing him, loving him, he knew he had to do something he hadn't done in a very long time.

He had to believe. In her. In them. In the future.

"I know we'll make it work. I'm sure of it."

A few more tears spilled over her cheeks and she leaned into him. He wrapped his arm around her, holding her tight and close. Because she had given him that. The ability to believe again. The ability of certainty in her love. She had given him so many of the things he'd lost.

"Move in with me."

She jerked away and looked up at him with wide eyes. "What?"

"Move in with me. We'll start building that future."

"That's awfully sudden," she said in a hushed tone, but her hand was still in his, her body still so close, her eyes searching for something on his face.

He laughed. "You start from the beginning, and it's hardly sudden."

"But you didn't know me. I was just email."

"It was the truth. I think it was your heart as much as I know it was mine."

She looked at him in wonder and then she smiled. Wide and beautiful. "Yeah. I think you're right. I think you're right. Move in with you, huh?"

"Just think, you'll be this close to Gallagher's. Plus you can help me weed."

"I can watch you weed from the porch."

He laughed. "Good enough. That'll be more than good enough." He bent his mouth to hers. "Is that a yes?"

She swallowed, and there were more tears welling there, but he was certain—sure—they were happy tears.

"That's a yes."

So, he kissed her with all the hope and certainty and belief she'd given him.

And now . . .
Read on for a preview of
NEED YOU NOW
A Mile High Romance
by
Nicole Helm

*Only the most resilient of souls could breathe new life into an all-but-forgotten town nestled in the shadow of the Rocky Mountains—but what they get in return might be worth the heartache it takes to make it happen . . .*

Gracely, Colorado, was once a booming mining town. No one knows that better than Brandon Evans. His father's company kept the town thriving for years—until Brandon threatened to expose his illegal practices and drove him away. Everyone blames Brandon and his brother for turning Gracely into a ghost town—but the tenacious residents cling to a long-held legend about the land's healing powers. And Brandon has a plan to spin that legend into reality . . .

Lilly Preston took a leap of faith and moved to Gracely a year ago to save her nephew from an abusive situation. She would do anything for him, even sacrifice her glamorous job. Reluctantly, the former PR hot shot takes a job at the ruggedly handsome Evans brothers' Mile High Adventures, a company offering restorative Rocky Mountain vacations.

Brandon thinks PR is pointless, and Lilly knows less than nothing about the outdoors. Which is exactly why they need each other—in ways neither ever imagined . . .

Available in June 2017 wherever books and ebooks are sold.

# Chapter 1

Brandon Evans stood on the deck outside his office and stared at the world below him, a kaleidoscope of browns and greens and grays, all the way down the mountain until the rooftops of Gracely, Colorado, dotted the view.

Across the valley, up the other side of the jagged stone mountain, the deserted Evans Mining Corporation buildings stood like ghosts—haunting him and his family. A glaring reminder of the destruction he'd wrought while trying to do the right thing.

He wished it were a cloudy day so he couldn't see the damn things, but he'd built the headquarters of his company where it was so he could remind himself what he was fighting for. What was right.

"Are you over there being broody?"

Brandon looked down at his mug of coffee balanced on the porch railing, not bothering to glance at his brother. He *was* brooding. He was being outvoted, and he didn't like it. He took a sip of coffee, now cool from the chilled spring air.

He leveled a gaze at his brother, Will, and their business partner, Sam. This was his best *I'm a leader* look, and it usually worked.

Why the hell wasn't it working today?

"Hiring a PR consultant goes against everything we're trying to do." Of course, he'd already explained that and he'd still been outvoted.

"We need help. The town isn't going to learn to forgive us. We can do all the good in the world, but without someone actually making inroads—we're not getting anywhere. We can't even find a receptionist from Gracely. No one will acknowledge we *exist*."

"We have Skeet."

"Skeet is not a receptionist. He's a-a-help me out here, Sam?"

"His name is *Skeet*," Sam replied, as if that explained everything.

The grizzled old man who answered the phones for their outdoor adventure excursion company and refused to use a computer *was* a bit of a problem, but he worked cheap and he was a local. Brandon had been adamant about hiring only locals.

Of course, Skeet was a local that everyone shunned, and he seemed to speak only in grunts, but they'd yet to lose an interested customer.

That they knew of, as Will liked to point out.

Brandon set the cold coffee down on the railing of the deck. He needed to do something with his hands. He couldn't sit still—he was too frustrated that they were standing around arguing instead of Sam and Will jumping to do his bidding.

Why had he thought to make them all equal partners?

"She's local. Great experience with a firm in Denver. She can be just what we need to turn the tide." Will ticked off the points they'd already been over, patient as ever.

"She's *recently* local—not a native—and she can't change our last name."

"Well, even if we had lifelong townies working at Mile High that wouldn't happen."

"Can we cut the bullshit?" Sam interrupted. "You were outvoted, Brandon. She's hired. Now I've got to go."

"You don't have a group to guide until two."

Sam was already inside the cabin that acted as their office, the words probably never reaching him. Apparently his time-around-other-humans allotment was up for the morning. Not that shocking. The fact that they'd lured him from his hermit mountain cabin before a guided hike was unusual.

Brandon turned his stare to his brother. They were twins. Born five minutes apart, but the five minutes had always felt like years. He was a typical older brother, and any time Sam sided with Will, Brandon couldn't help but get his nose a little out of joint.

He was the responsible, business-minded one, not the in-for-a-good-time playboy. They should listen to him regardless, he thought. Brandon had spearheaded Mile High Adventures. It was his baby, his penance, his hope of offering Gracely some healing in the wake of his father's mess. The fact that Will and Sam sometimes disagreed with him about the best way to do that filled him with a dark energy, and he needed to do something physical to burn it off.

"Go chop some wood. Build a birdhouse. Climb a mountain for all I care. She'll be here at ten. Be back by then," Will ordered.

"You know I'd just as soon throat punch you as do what you tell me to do."

Will grinned. "Oh, brother, if I kept my mouth shut every time you wanted to throat punch me, I'd never speak."

"Uh-huh."

Will's expression went grave, which was always a bad sign. They both dealt with weighty things and emotion differently—Brandon acted like a dick and Will acted like nothing mattered. If Will was acting like something was important . . .

Well, shit.

"Don't think we don't take it seriously," Will said, far too quietly for Brandon's comfort. "Trust, every once in a while, that we know as much or more than you."

"My ass," Brandon grumbled, feeling at least a little ashamed.

"She'll be here at ten. I have that spring break group at ten thirty, and you, lucky man, don't have anything on your plate today. Which means you get to be in charge of paper—"

"Don't say it."

"—work and orientation!" Will concluded all too jovially.

"I could probably throw you off the mountain and no one would ask any questions."

"Ah, but then who would take the bachelorette parties since you and Sam refuse?" Will clapped him on the shoulder. "You'll like her. She's got that business-tunnel-vision thing down that you do so well."

Brandon took a page out of Skeet's book and merely grunted, which Will—thank god—took as a cue to leave.

Regardless of whether or not he'd like this Lilly Preston, Brandon didn't see the usefulness in hiring a PR consultant. What was that going to accomplish when the town already hated them?

If even Will's personality couldn't win people over, they were toast in that department. The only thing that was going to sway people's minds was an economically booming town. Mile High had a long way to go to make Gracely boom. And they needed the town's help.

Hiring someone who had only cursory knowledge of Gracely lore, who couldn't possibly understand what they were trying to do, wasn't the answer. Worse, it reeked of something his father would have done when he was trying to hide all the shady business practices he'd instituted at Evans Mining.

Brandon glanced back over at the empty buildings. If he wanted to, he could will away the memories, the images in his mind. The pristine hallways, the steady buzz of phones and conversation. How much he'd wanted that to be *his* one day.

But then he'd told his father he knew what was going on, and if Dad didn't change, Brandon would have no choice but to go to the authorities.

The fallout had been the Evans Mining headquarters leaving Gracely after more than a century of being the heart of the town, his father's subsequent heart attack and death, Mom shutting them out, and everything about his life as the golden child and heir apparent to the corporation imploding before his very eyes.

A lot of consequences for the one tiny domino he'd flicked when his conscience couldn't take the possible outcomes of his father's shady business practices.

So much work to do to make it right. He forced his gaze away from those buildings to the mountains all around him. He took a deep breath of the thin air scented with heavy pine. He rubbed his palms over the rough wood of the deck railing.

It was his center—these mountains, this place. He believed he could bring this town back to life not just because he owed it to the residents who'd treated him like a king growing up, but because there was something . . . elemental about these mountains, this sky, the river tributaries, and the animals that lived within it all.

Untouched, ethereal, and while he didn't exactly believe in the magic and ghostly legends of Gracely's healing power, he did believe in these mountains and this air. He was going to give his all to fix the damage he'd caused, and he was going to give his all to making Mile High Adventures everything it could be.

So, he'd put up with this unwanted PR woman for the few weeks it would take to prove that Will and Sam were wrong. Once they admitted he was right, they could move on to the next thing, and the next thing, until they got exactly what they wanted.

Lilly took a deep, cleansing breath of the mountain air. The altitude was much higher up here than in the little valley Gracely was nestled into, but even aside from that, the office of Mile High Adventures was breathtaking.

It was like something out of a brochure—which should make her job easier. A cabin nestled into the side of a mountain; all dark logs and green trimmed roof, with a snow-peaked top of a mountain settled right behind to complete the look of cozy mountain getaway. The porches were almost as big as the cabin itself. She'd suggest some colorful deck chairs, a few fire pits to complete the look, but it took no imagination at all to picture groups of people and mugs of hot chocolate and colorful plaid blankets.

The sign next to the door that read MILE HIGH ADVENTURES was carved into a wood plank that matched the logs of the cabin.

If it weren't for the men who ran this company, she'd be crying with relief and excitement. She *needed* a job that would allow her to stay in Gracely, and this one would pay enough that she could still support her sister and nephew even with Cora's dwindling waitress hours and low tips.

Cora and Micah were doing so well, finally moving on from the abusive nightmare that had been Stephen. Lilly couldn't uproot them, and she couldn't leave them. They needed her, but her Denver-based PR company had refused to let her continue to work remotely when they'd merged with another company and only kept those employees willing to relocate to Denver.

So here she was, about to agree to work for the kind of men she couldn't stand. Rich, entitled, charming. The kind of men who'd hurt her mother, her sister, her nephew.

Lilly forced herself to step forward. This was work, not romance, so it didn't matter. She'd do her job, take their money, do her best to improve the light in which their business was seen in Gracely, and not let any of these rich and powerful men touch her.

Shoulders back, she walked up the stairs of the porch. There was a sign on the door, hung from a nail and string. It read *Come On In!* in flowing script. She imagined if she flipped the sign there'd be some kind of WE'RE CLOSED phrase on the back.

Impressive detail for a group of three burly mountain men who were, from what she could tell, hated by the town at large.

Her stomach jittered, cramped. She really didn't want to do this. She *loved* Gracely. Even with all its problems, it was charming and calming. She felt cozy and comfortable here. More than she'd ever felt in Denver, where she'd grown up.

Working for Mile High would keep her here, but would it still be cozy and comfortable if the town looked at her with contempt? If they considered her tainted by association with these men she'd never heard a good word about?

Well, as long as Cora and Micah still needed her, it didn't matter. Couldn't.

She blew out a breath and lifted a steady hand. She opened the door. Will *had* instructed her to come on in, and the sign said the same.

Upon stepping into an open area that seemed designed as both lobby and living room, she wasn't surprised to find more wood, a crackling fire in the fireplace, warm and worn brown leather couches around the hearth. The walls were mostly bare, but there was a deer head over the mantel and a few framed graphics with quotes about going to the mountains and the wilderness.

A grunt caused Lilly to jerk her attention to the big desk opposite the entryway. She wasn't sure what she'd expected of the other employees of Mile High, but she'd assumed they'd all be like Will. Young, athletic, charming, and handsome.

The man sitting behind the desk was *none* of those things. He was small and old with a white beard and a white ponytail. A bit of a Willie Nelson/*Bad Santa*-looking character in a stained Marine Corps sweatshirt.

Not what she expected of a receptionist . . . anywhere.

"Hello. My name is Lilly Preston. I'm supposed to be meeting Will Evans and his broth—"

The man grunted again, a sound that was a gravelly huff and seemed to shake his entire small frame.

What on earth was happening?

"Ah, Lilly!" Will appeared from a hallway in the back. "Skeet, you're not scaring off our newest employee, are you?"

The man—Skeet, good lord—grunted again. Maybe he was their . . . grandfather or something.

She returned her attention and polite business smile to Will and the man behind him. It wasn't any stretch to realize this was Will's brother, Brandon Evans. There were a lot of similarities: their height, the dark brown hair—though Brandon's was short and Will's was long enough to have a bit of a wave to it. They both had varying levels of beard, hazel eyes, and the kind of angular, masculine face one would definitely associate with men who climbed mountains and kayaked rivers for a living.

There were some key differences—mainly, Will was smiling, all straight white teeth. Brandon's mouth was formed in something a half inch away from a scowl.

Well. She forced her smile to go wider and more pleasant. She wasn't a novice at dealing with cranky or difficult men. About seventy-five percent of her career thus far had included dealing with obstinate and opinionated business owners. The Evans brothers might be different, but they weren't unique.

"You have an absolutely lovely office. I'm so impressed."

Will gestured her toward the couches around the fireplace. There were rugs over the hardwood floor, patterns of dark red and green and brown. It was no lie, she *was* impressed.

"Have a seat, Lilly. I have a group to guide rock climbing shortly, so Brandon will conduct most of your orientation. We've got the necessary paperwork." He placed a stack of papers on the rough-hewn wood coffee table. It looked like it had probably come from Annie's—the furniture shop in Gracely. Furnishing and decorating from local vendors would be smart.

Smart, rich men with charming smiles and handsome scowls. It didn't get much more dangerous than that, but Lilly never let her smile falter.

"Once we've done that, Brandon will show you around, show you your desk, and you can ask any questions."

"Of course." She leaned forward to take the paperwork, but Brandon's hand all but slapped on top of the stack.

"One thing first," Brandon said.

Will muttered something that sounded like an expletive.

The stomach jittering/cramping combo was back, but she refused to let it show on her face. Nerves were normal, and the way she always dealt with them was to ignore them through the pleasantest smiles and friendliest chitchat she could manage until they went away.

"I'm at your disposal, Mr. Evans," she said, letting her hand fall away from the papers as she settled comfortably into the couch. At least she hoped she was exuding the appearance of comfort.

His expression, which hadn't been all that friendly or welcoming, darkened even further. "You will call me Brandon. You will call him Will. There are no misters here."

Ah, so he was one of those. Determined to be an everyman. She resisted an eye roll.

He leaned forward, hazel eyes blazing into hers. "Do you believe in the legend, Ms. Preston?"

"The . . . legend?" This was not what she'd expected. At all. She quickly glanced at the door in her periphery. Maybe she should bolt.

"You've lived here how long? Surely you've heard the legend of Gracely."

"You mean . . ." She hesitated because she didn't know where he was trying to lead her, and she didn't like going into uncharted territory. But he seemed adamant, so she continued. "The one that says those who choose Gracely as their home will find the healing their heart desires?"

"Is there another?"

Lilly had to tense to keep the pleasant smile on her face. She didn't like the way this Evans brother spoke to her. Like he was an interrogating detective. Like she'd done something wrong, when Will had been the one to convince her to take this job.

Because working with the Evanses was going to put a big red X on her back in town, and she didn't trust men like them with their centuries of good breeding and money.

But she needed a job. She needed to stay in Gracely. So she had to ignore the way his tone put her back up and smile pleasantly and pretend he wasn't being a giant asshat.

"So, Ms. Preston." Oh she hated the way he *drawled* her name. "The question is: Do you believe in the legend?"

This was a test, a blatant one, and yet . . . she didn't know the right answer. Would he ridicule her for believing in fairy tales if she said she believed the first settlers of Gracely were magically healed when they settled here and all the stories that had been built up into legend since? Would he take issue with her being cynical and hard if she said there was no way?

The biggest problem was her answer existed somewhere in between the two. Half of her thought it was foolishness. Losing her job and having to take this one hardly seemed like good luck, but her sister and nephew had flourished here in the past year and, well, healing was possible. Magic? Maybe—maybe not. But possible.

So, maybe it was best to focus on the good, the possibility. "Yes." She met his penetrating hazel gaze, keeping her expression the picture-perfect blank slate of professional politeness.

"And what do you think is the source of that legend? What makes it true?"

"True?" She looked at Will, tried to catch his gaze, but he looked at the ceiling. She might not trust Will, but at least he was polite. Apparently also a giant coward.

"Yes, if you believe Gracely can heal, what do you believe *causes* that ability?"

She flicked her gaze back to his. It had never wavered. There was a fierceness to his expression that made her nervous. He was a big man. Tall, broad. Though he wore a thick sweater and heavy work pants and boots, it was fairly obvious that beneath all those layers was a man who could probably crush her with one arm.

She suddenly felt very small and very vulnerable. Weak and at a disadvantage.

Which was just the kind of thing she wouldn't show them. Powerful men got off on causing fear and vulnerability. She'd seen her nephew's father do that enough to have built a mask against it, and she'd worked with and for plenty of men who'd wanted to intimidate her for a variety of reasons.

She could handle whatever this was. Chin up. Spine straight. A practiced down-the-nose look. "Do legends need a cause? A scientific explanation? Or are they simply . . . magic? Do I need to analyze *why* I believe in it, or can I simply believe it happened and continues to? And furthermore, what on earth does it have to do with my work here?"

"If you're going to work here," he said, his voice low and . . . fierce to match his face, "you will need to understand what *we* believe about the legend. Because it has everything to do with why we built Mile High Adventures."

"That's not what I heard," she muttered before she could stop herself. Okay, maybe remote consulting *had* dulled some of her instincts if she let that slip out.

"Oh, and what did you hear, Ms. Preston? That we're the evil spawn of Satan setting out to crush Gracely even deeper into the earth? That we're bringing in an influx of out-of-towners, not to *help* the businesses of Gracely, but to piss off the natives? Because if you think we don't know what this town thinks of us, you don't understand why you're here."

"I know what the town thinks of you *and* I know why I'm here." She took a deep breath, masked with a smile, of course. "I'm here because I think this is an excellent opportunity." *To sell my soul briefly so I can stay where I want.* "I do believe in the legend, and I think it would be imperative you do too if you expect to sell the town on you being part of its salvation."

His eyes narrowed and she knew she was skating on thin ice. He was one of those control freaks who didn't like to be told what to do, but unlike most of the men she'd worked with, he wasn't placated by sweet smiles or politeness.

She'd have to find a new tactic.

"I believe, Ms. Preston"—that damn conceited drawl again—"in these mountains. In this *air*. I believe that if people choose to look, they can find themselves here. I believe in this town, and that it can be more than what it's become. You'll need to believe that too if you want to work here."

"We've already hired her, Brandon," Will said, *finally* inserting something into the conversation. *After* letting this man act as though she were . . . unwelcome, unwanted.

Typical.

"*You* hired her."

"Did I walk into the middle of something, gentlemen? I can come back at another time when you're ready to be in agreement." She stood, picking up her bag and sliding it over her shoulder. She might be desperate, but she wasn't going to sell half her soul *and* be treated poorly.

This was not what she'd signed up for. She'd just as soon move back to Denver. It would kill her to leave Cora and Micah, but she had some pride she couldn't swallow.

"Have a seat, Ms. Preston."

When she raised an eyebrow at Brandon the Bastard, he pressed his lips together, then released a sigh. "If you would, please," he said through gritted teeth.

Ugh. Men.

She took a seat. One more chance. He had *one* more chance.

"I apologize if I've come off . . ."

Will spoke up. "Harsh. Douchey. Asshole spectacular."

Brandon glared at his brother, who was grinning. She didn't want to find it humorous. They were both being spectacular assholes as far as she was concerned, just in different ways.

"This business, what it stands for, it's everything to me, so I don't take it lightly."

She met Brandon's gaze. Just as she didn't want to find him amusing, she didn't want to soften, but she realized in that simple, gravely uttered sentence, that he wasn't fierce so much as . . .

Passionate.

She met his gaze with that realization and her stomach did something other than the alternating jittery cramps. Her chest seemed to expand—something flipped, like when Cora drove them too fast down a mountain road.

She couldn't put her finger on that. The cause, what it was, and more, she didn't think she wanted to. If she was going to survive working for the Evans brothers, it was probably best to keep her polite smile in place and ignore any and all *feelings*.

**Nicole Helm** grew up with her nose in a book and a dream of becoming a writer. Nicole writes down-to-earth contemporary romance. From farmers to cowboys, Midwest to the West, she writes stories about people finding themselves and finding love in the process. When she's not writing, she spends her time dreaming about someday owning a barn. She lives with her husband and two young sons in Missouri.